Beautiful Men

20 Stories that will Heal your Soul,
Ignite your Passion, and Inspire your Divine Purpose

Foreword By Former President Obama White House
Fatherhood *Champion of Change* and Representative

THABITI BOONE

7 House Media

7 House Media
www.7housemedia.com
Atlanta, GA

Editor: Sherman Turntine
Jennifer Wilkes
Cover Design: Saba Tekle

The Author of this book does not dispense medical advice or prescribe the use of any technique as a form of treatment for physical or medical problems Without the advice of a physician. The intent of the author is only to offer information of a general nature and to help you in your quest for emotional and physical Well-being. In the event you use any of the information in this book yourself, which is your constitutional right, the author & publisher assume no responsibility for your actions.

Printed in the United States
10 9 8 7 6 5 4 3 2 1

CONTENTS

Introduction

Before there was *"20 Beautiful Men,"* there were *"20 Beautiful Women."* The original series started off as a book and has evolved into so much more. Not only was it featured in The Huffington Post, HLN's "The Daily Share" and BuzzFeed, as well as many other media outlets, it also inspired the #20BeautifulWomen Challenge, in which over a million women participated. It is now a global movement advancing sisterhood, a blog section in The Huffington Post, and the subject of an upcoming documentary.

Since the release of Volume 1, there have been men asking, "What about us?" So here we are with Volume 1 of the new book series focusing on men and their individual stories of healing, passion and purpose.

There is so much more to come, but first let's start with how this all began...

Most of my life I lived in pain, and one of my deepest pains was feeling I was alone. When I would open up about my troubles to friends, I would either experience them not caring or them sharing what I wanted to keep secret. Although I had family, sometimes I needed someone outside of my family to help me. This void would make me feel like I had no one to turn to at times but God. God's grace guided me to empowering books.

Each book I read helped my healing process because of the author's courage and vulnerability to share things that I learned to keep hidden. My beautiful soul and spiritual sisters, Iyanla Vanzant, Marianne Williamson and Lisa Nichols, to name a few, empowered me and taught me so much. They allowed me to see that I was never alone.

I began to see that people were good at masking their pain, and I was able to connect more dots.

Many of us hide parts of our lives, learning early on to tuck the ugly pains away with hopes that people won't be able to see are true selves.

We've learned to look good on the outside, creating the ability to flawlessly hide parts of ourselves. This causes us to die on the inside, yet barely existing, we still call this "living." Our souls and spirits wither every day we walk in an inauthentic manner, disillusioned of what a perfect person or perfect life is.

But through the midst of darkness and confusion, I have brought 20 beautiful men together to share their stories and now 20 beautiful men rise to meet the challenge. Twenty beautiful men stand together, exposing their imperfections, their emotional scars and wounds — wounds that have shaped them and inspired them to do the work they do for people today.

A beautiful man shares his story
so other men and women won't feel alone.
A beautiful man is peaceful:
He has made peace with his past.
A beautiful man is passionate:
He is on fire with a strong desire to change the world.
A beautiful man is purposeful:
He knows why he was born
and does what he was created to do.

Be Beautiful,

Saba Tekle

FOREWORD

Have we come far enough as a society to define men as "beautiful?" Can being beautiful as men provide a deeper understanding than physical appearance?

20 Beautiful Men helps answer those questions. It takes us out of our comfort zone into a deeper appreciation that men, too, can be seen and told they're beautiful – the kind of beautiful that's rooted in the souls of all men.

When I received a call from Saba asking if I would write the foreword, I asked her to please give me a few days to think about it. I thought writing on this particular subject would be quite challenging.

As I read the introduction on what drove her spirit and vision, along with reviewing the inspiring stories by some incredible men, I told her I would be honored to write the foreword.

What she didn't realize was that by giving me the opportunity to write the foreword, she also provided me the opportunity to tap into my own soul and reflect on my passion and purpose. I needed to ask myself, "For all I've done and been through in my life, *am I beautiful?"*

We are all born with a life that we may perceive as perfect and beautiful. Some of us are born with the gift of love from our parents. That love can transform into a foundation of feeling beautiful about ourselves and the anticipation of a world that awaits and embraces who we are. *To feel beautiful is to have the ultimate feeling of being free in the space of our likeness, passion, and purpose.*

Of course, this feeling may immediately change once we leave our home and when the forces of other people's pain encroach on our lives. We may then begin to attack our self-worth, our self-esteem, and the values we place on ourselves, which may deter our divine path or the plans we've set for our lives.

Not all of us are so lucky to come from a home filled with love. The circumstances of the world I was born into weren't so beautiful. That world was quite ugly. I was born to a mother who became pregnant with me at the age of 13 by a 21-year-old, street-hustler – my father. As a little boy, I had a front row seat as I watched the only affection my father ever showed toward my mother was by beating on her on a regular basis. I never saw the hugs, kisses, and playful moments between my parents. I don't have many memories of my sister, brother, and I enjoying our parents as a family.

I do remember the loud noise at night coming from their bedroom. I would lie in my bed, too afraid to go to sleep, imagining what my mother would look like in the morning from the damage done by my father. There were some mornings I would look at my mother's scars. She did her best to hide the pain on her face as she prepared me for school. She always had a faraway look as if to disconnect herself from the reality of being less than 20 years old, going from seventh grade to motherhood, being in an abusive marriage, accepting government welfare, and living a life of hopelessness.

I believe my dad wanted to be a good father, but he just didn't know how. He grew up with so much pain in his own life. As a little boy, his mother, whom he loved dearly, passed away. Equally devastating was the day he lost his hand at work when a meat grinder accidentally turned on while he was washing the machine. To compensate for his emotional pain and physical disability, my dad developed a very street-tough, angry persona as a way to protect and defend himself.

One of his weapons was a steel hook he wore to substitute his left hand. I've seen my father hurt people with his left-hand hook. His other weapon was a gun he kept on his hip.

He soon became a well-known street hustler, gambler, womanizer, abusive husband, and neglectful father. He was someone who didn't believe in the legitimate and traditional 9 to 5 employment lifestyle or healthy family relationships and activities.

Nicknamed JB, his anger brought terror to my mother as well as those who crossed his path.

If being born into a distressed home wasn't enough, add on growing up in one of the toughest neighborhoods in New York City ravaged by drugs, crime, violence, gangs, and poverty. There weren't too many beautiful things to see in the 'hood. A boy or man could never be seen as having any so-called beautiful qualities. There were consequences for being too nice, a gentleman, or a man who protected and cared for his children, women, and family.

The irony of the 'hood was that the *harder* you were and the more abusive you were to others, the more credibility you gained in the streets. As boys, we were taught *the man code* – not to show any emotions... "Stop acting like a b*tch! Stop crying like a b*tch!" If you were caught crying, your self-esteem would be challenged and destroyed. Boys and men were taught that having a heart and soul was a sign of weakness. And in my 'hood, weakness could get you killed.

Then came the moment! At the age of 12, on a sunny Sunday afternoon, I was at the neighborhood playground honing my skills and NBA dreams on the basketball court. I was seen as being the next rising star who could make it to the big league.

One of my friends ran onto the court and yelled, "Your mother is at the top of the rooftop housing project!" As I was still dribbling and playing, I wasn't sure what I had just heard. He yelled again, "Your mother is in the back of the building on the ledge of the rooftop!" I immediately dropped the basketball.

I ran a block and a half toward the back of our building. As I was turning the corner looking up, my mother came crashing down on the grass. It was a loud *thud!* I stood over her as blood poured out of her mouth and both of her legs were twisted and broken. We locked eyes, not sure if it would be the last look between us. My body went completely numb.

Death wouldn't have her. She survived.

As I watched the woman who gave birth to me jump off a six-story building, I wasn't sure if I had died that day. A few years later, the only person who I considered to be the most beautiful thing in the world, my grandmother, had passed away.

Adding up all the emotional trauma I had experienced at only 14 years old, I will never forget the amount of anger and pain I felt.

How could God give me such a bad deal? How would I be able to handle the impact of these early experiences? The world became very ugly.

I had a hard time associating with things and people most call "beautiful." My soul, my purpose became homeless. The only thing I had was my basketball, my determination, and my dreams.

I dribbled around all the obstacles and challenges that got in my way, including becoming a single parent at 19. Doing the unthinkable, thanks to my basketball scholarship, I arrived on a college campus with my book bag, basketball, and baby. I gained national attention for defying the odds, graduating from college, and sacrificing my NBA dreams to raise my daughter.

Over the years, I've had a lot of success and achievements, but I still felt unfulfilled. There was pain blocking me from becoming the real me. I needed to find Thabiti – to find validation and acceptance.

In 2007, a collision of two worlds would begin to head in the same direction and end up at the same destiny of purpose. I became a CNN Hero for Championing Children the same year that Barack Hussein Obama announced his candidacy for president of the United States.

The man who was on a pilgrimage in search of himself and a boy who hardly new his father would later become our country's first Black president.

As if time could stand still long enough for my past to catch up, enduring my own fatherhood pain, I became one of President Obama's White House Fatherhood Champions of Change. President Obama was not only the most powerful leader in the world but one of the most beautiful human beings I have ever met and had the pleasure of serving and representing.

I always felt that my pain and purpose were held hostage inside my mother. From the time she became pregnant with me, her abuse, suicide attempt, sadness, and self-hatred became who I was. We were both trapped. The only way I was to free myself was to free my mother. Bringing out the beauty in her would release the beautiful soul and purpose within me. There were few things my mother and I shared together. I couldn't seem to make her proud of me.

God put in my spirit one final chance. I knew how much my mother loved President Obama. I called her with one final appeal to join me at the president's last White House Holiday Reception. She agreed.

Before she could change her mind, I arranged for her travel and hotel accommodations. My family was excited and helped get her prepared for the trip. Her new dress and hairstyle were all set.

As I walked her into the White House, I began to see and feel her spirit. She was glowing. Her personality lit up everyone. As the President walked towards her, she started shaking knowing she was finally meeting him. President Obama hugged her and told her how beautiful she was. The President, knowing that was my mother, looked at me and said, "Thank you for serving me, my administration, and our country." I said, "Mr. President, it was an honor to serve as your Fatherhood Champion." My mother needed to hear those words of affirmation. More importantly, she needed to hear the President of the United States acknowledge her son.

That night at the White House, God used President Obama to free two souls. I was reintroduced to my mother. She and I finally became mother and son, hugging, talking, and enjoying one another. We were able to release the darkness of our past and openly demonstrate the love we both needed. Seeing how beautiful my mother was, I saw the beautiful man who was inside of me.

All along, it was my pain driving my purpose. That's why this book is so timely and critical. *20 Beautiful Men* is about men releasing themselves. It is important for men to share, heal, and connect with our souls.

I applaud Saba for taking on this heroic literary work offering men a platform and the men for opening up their lives sharing their stories of pain, insecurities, vulnerability, adversity, redemption, triumphs, self-discovery, the power of love, and relationships to find their space of truth.

It speaks to her character and the unselfishness of her womanliness to go beyond herself and cultural stereotypes to uplift men. It wasn't enough for her to portray *20 Beautiful Women.* She wanted to make sure men received the same celebration of having beautiful souls as well. *What's more affirming than when women support men?*

The power of this book challenges society's notion of male masculinity. Societal culture has been the complete opposite. We are taught not to express our emotions and experience pain. This book allows men to confront the real definition of our manhood and purpose.

Each story is filled with men taking the reader on their respective journeys speaking from their own voices and their own authentic experiences. It is in their stories that we find our own story.

20 Beautiful Men is about connecting to our passion wrapped around our gifts, talents, aspirations, dreams, desires, and purpose.

We all must return to that place if we are not there already. Let this book be a guide for you now and the years to come.

Can you imagine how beautiful our women, children, families, and world can be when men are seen as beautiful?

I'm sure everyone who reads this book will walk away, as I have, inspired by the beauty that's in all of us.

- ***Thabiti Boone***

1

"The Awakened Man"

By Dan Mason

October 26, 2015.

I was in a fog as I walked down the long, sterile corporate hallway to retrieve my personal belongings from my office. It didn't matter that I just resigned from my high-salary, low-fulfillment radio executive job. It didn't matter that I would have been fired if I didn't resign first. It didn't matter I had run myself into the ground and felt completely uncertain about my future. At this moment, all that mattered was *freedom.*

Freedom from working for a company I didn't believe in. Freedom from waking up feeling lethargic and depleted, dreading another day running the hamster wheel at a job I should have never taken in the first place. Ultimately, it meant freedom to stop being what everyone else expected so I could finally evolve into the man I was meant to become.

The evolution couldn't happen by itself. It required me to dig deep and ask the one question every man must face if he is to grow into a fully realized version of himself:

Why had I spent my life trying to receive my value FROM the world, rather than bring my intrinsic value TO the world?

Over the previous twenty years, whenever people asked me about myself, my job was the first and sometimes the only thing I would talk about.

"I'm in radio!"

It was my one-dimensional, superficial battle cry – default answer to keep up the appearance of seeming important while simultaneously avoiding vulnerability and rejection. If I simply talked about *what I did*, I'd never have to open and share *who I was.*

My snarky, sarcastic, radio persona was rewarded with attention from listeners and unending social media likes. Behind a microphone, I felt in control. I could be loved for my wit without having to expose my wounds. People only knew the funny guy, not the man weakened by years of depression, people-pleasing, and a perpetual feeling of unworthiness.

People approached me on the street and said, "Hey, Dan. I heard what you said on the radio!" Strangers listened to me. They engaged with me. In some small way, I felt like my voice mattered. It was intoxicating for a guy who was rewarded as a child for being silent and not rocking the boat.

In my other role as a behind-the-scenes executive, I was praised as a creative leader with good instincts. I was known for delivering huge results in competitive situations other people considered unwinnable. Rewards came in the form of regular salary increases and bonus money, which provided me all the material things a naïve man believes gives him value. I bought a new Lexus at age 24 and bought a swanky condo the year after. I wore designer clothes, ate at the best restaurants, and took elaborate vacations. My life looked incredible on Facebook. By every measure, I was successful. Yet, I felt deeply unfulfilled and emotionally bankrupt. No matter what I achieved, it never felt like enough. I never felt like I was enough.

Thus, I spent my life outsourcing my worthiness to the world. The highs of validation, love, praise, and acceptance from other people become addicting to the man who does not understand how to give those things to himself.

For me, the short-term hit of significance felt great at the moment but never lasted. Like the alcoholic who woke up after a drinking binge with a headache and hangover, I would always come right back down from my "validation high" into a place of guilt and shame. The love I received felt inauthentic *because I was being inauthentic.* I wasn't being loved for who I was but for who the world wanted me to be.

Constantly pushing harder in my career to make my parents proud, putting my needs last in relationships to please a partner, and always striving to get more "stuff" to impress my friends, my self-worth was predicated on the acceptance of others. This is the recipe for a midlife crisis.

However, on this day, I would be forced to figure out a new path. The universe foreclosed on my safe, little patch of land in the corporate comfort zone. The mask of achievement had been removed, and I felt naked.

I quietly shut my office door and tried not to be noticed as I made my way to the elevator. The low-level hum of the florescent lights overhead synchronized with the low-level anxiety I felt building in the pit of my stomach.

I had 1000 different worst-case scenarios in my head, but they all boiled down to two fears:

First, what if I'm not enough as I am, without the bells and whistles of an "important" title?

Second, if I'm not enough, will people still love me?

Before I could answer these questions and create a new life built on purpose, I had to make peace with my past. I had to become the *Indiana Jones* of my psychology, unearthing clues to find the truth. *Was I born inadequate, or did I simply make a disempowering choice to feel that way?*

The answer was buried nearly thirty years in the past. It was May 1987:

I watched my mother smile from ear to ear as she took each trophy out of the box and placed it on our living room mantle. The awards recognized my extensive academic and social achievements during my sixth-grade year at Mayde Creek Junior High School in Texas.

There was an award for being voted most popular. Another trophy, adorned with gold basketballs and baseball bats honored me as the most athletic. A huge plaque recognized me as a top academic performer.

The icing on the cake? A trophy with a couple ballroom dancing on top declaring my girlfriend and me as the class couple. My mother couldn't wait to show these trophies off to her friends. However, there was one small problem. I never really accomplished any of those things.

My mom went to a local trophy store and paid to have the awards created. She made up a fake narrative about the school year to compete with the other mothers she knew in what felt like the most bizarre "Real Housewives" storyline ever.

The truth was way less exciting. I was a wallflower who struggled to make connections. I had braces and a bad haircut. The transition from a private K-5 elementary school to a public junior high school was brutal. I didn't have many friends. I was bullied endlessly in the locker room and dreaded gym class. The girlfriend was nonexistent. I was too shy to even talk to girls.

But as I watched my mother brag and show off my "awards" to her friends, 11-year-old Dan made a decision.

Whoever I was that year wasn't enough for my mother to be proud of. I needed to be more.

I don't remember making this decision consciously. Then again, our most disempowering choices are never made from a place of high emotional awareness.

At that moment, the overachiever was born. I began a 25-year quest to be the kind of person my mother could be proud of. The most logical starting point was to be more like my father. While my friends enjoyed summer vacations by the pool, I would set my alarm for 6 a.m. and go to work with dad, learning the radio business from the ground up.

By age sixteen, I had my first on-air job reading the news and sports reports for a little AM radio station nobody listened to. By age 21, I graduated college and took a job as a program director and nighttime DJ at a small station in Maine. Within 18 months, I was running a major market radio station in Cleveland. From there, it was off to chase the "next big thing" from Miami to Sacramento to Boston and Tampa…

And then I landed at rock bottom.

After 27 years, I felt tired, depressed, and uninspired. I had invested so many years creating a life that would please my family and make me worthy of all those trophies; I completely abandoned myself in the process.

It's also one of the greatest gifts I've been given.

Getting lost was a necessary detour for me to ultimately find my way home. It showed me the path to reconnect with my higher self and learn the deeper truth of what it meant to be a man. The hundreds of lessons along the journey changed me, but three, in particular, were most valuable:

A beautiful man understands fulfillment cannot be found by focusing on what he can get from life; it's about what he gives.

A beautiful man discovers his purpose, then aligns every aspect of his life with it so he may live with integrity.

A beautiful man does not slip into fear, judgement, or blame when he stumbles on his path.

For most of my life, I blamed my mother and my childhood for the years of low self-esteem. Today, I see the big picture. My mother never bought those trophies because she thought I was inadequate. *She bought them because she felt inadequate.*

As a high school dropout, the only gift she felt she could offer to the world was to be a mother. She wanted to be the best at it but didn't know how. My grandparents weren't particularly good role models. My mom did the best she could with the little awareness she had.

It's crazy to think that by age forty a human being has lived over 21 million minutes. Over that time, we make hundreds of millions of decisions – some of them consciously, but most of them unconsciously. During a fleeting three-minute span in 1986, a mother handed off the relay baton of unworthiness to her young son. Not knowing any better, the boy ran as hard as he could for as far as he could until he collapsed.

When I dusted myself off and got back on my feet, I was finally a man.

I walked into the world with new priorities and a purpose statement for my life I had scribbled in a notebook:

I was born to feel the authenticity which comes from myself and my higher power, and to feel the connection which results from inspiring others to feel the same.

For the first time, I saw all of myself. I knew who I was, where I had strayed, and how I could serve others who were still searching. From that place, insecurity and self-loathing were replaced with profound peace and self-respect.

I may have referred to myself as a "radio broadcaster," but my real identity exists in the multitudes under the surface; a communicator, storyteller, content creator, friend, motivator, leader, empathizer, spiritual seeker, mentor, a creative force, and so many other incredible qualities that continue to emerge from within each day.

Today, I take those gifts that made me successful in corporate America and use them in a way that allows me to contribute to the world, rather than consume from the world. As I work with men and women around the globe helping them connect to their bigger purpose, I feel fulfilled and connected to my own purpose.

A man defined by a job title will only see limited possibilities for his life. An awakened man's possibilities are as infinite as his own spirit.

....

BIO

Based in St. Petersburg, Florida, Dan Mason is a personal transformation catalyst, keynote speaker, blogger, and a supporter of the courageous. He has helped clients in seven countries get unstuck and discover their life purpose. His mission is to empower clients to create more love, passion, creativity, fulfillment, and joy in all aspects of their life.

www.creativesoulcoaching.net
dan@creativesoulcoaching.net
www.facebook.com/CSoulCoaching
@CSCDanMason

2

Our Beautiful (Yet Imperfect) Life Story

By Lionell Dixon

I'm a firm believer in the idea that the challenges we encounter in life are formulated for a reason. You and I are the ones who define that reason, which eventually leads us to our purpose. The choices we'll make as a result point us in a direction in which we'll meet our fates. Wisdom teaches us that no one is ever guaranteed a perfect life at birth. In fact, imperfections come at the costs of living.

I'm sure that everyone has past experience with things that may have appeared to be beyond their control. For me, it was my experience growing up without my father. I never asked him not to be there nor did I ask for all of the other misfortunes in my life. But, what I had to realize was that I could no longer use my past as an excuse for not being able to move on with my life. Instead, I learned to use my past as a lesson to help create the best possible future moving forward.

I was born on Feb. 4, 1984, at Newcomb Hospital in Vineland, New Jersey, to Caroline Dixon and George Smith. It was a month just before New York University student Rick Rubin and promoter manager Russell Simmons founded Def Jam Recordings together. My mom was fairly young when she gave birth to me at just 19 years old. My father had just turned 39 years old a month and a half after my birth.

We lived in Atlantic City, New Jersey, as a family for a short period of time. Then, after years of disagreements, my parents separated when I was 6 years old. We spent time bunking up with family members, friends, and even spent days at a time in a local shelter.

For some reason, it appeared as though my dad didn't want anything to do with us anymore.

My childhood was pretty rough because my mom was left alone to care for not just my brother and I but for a new addition to our family. Three days before my 8th birthday, my mom gave birth to a beautiful baby girl, my sister Shannon. Shannon had a different father who, not long after she was born, bailed out and never returned during the course of my childhood. Work was pretty unstable for my mom leaving us to depend on assistance from the government and church.

As a result of our family's misfortune, some of my classmates and neighborhood kids found a way to use this against us. It wasn't before long that I had to figure out a way to develop thick skin in order to look past all of the mockery, name-calling, and bullying. But I still never fully accepted, nor understood, why my peers had to be as cruel as they were toward those who weren't completely like them. On many occasions, my mom made sure to encourage me that it was okay to be different. She often said that trying to fit in sometimes is not always what it's *cracked up to be.*

In life, it's natural to secure the need to fit in socially. It gives us a sense of importance, which also satisfies the ego and boosts our self-esteem. I am the first to admit that being a loner is not a pleasant experience. I've personally had my share of this, which may be the reason why my peers mistreated me the way they did. I believe that the act of bullying somehow insinuates evidence of insecurities within a person. Trust me, where I come from there was a lot of that. Admittedly, my family could have experienced worst in comparison to others in the *hood.* One of the most valuable lessons that I learned was to maintain my faith in God and to stay true to myself.

But it was during my early teenage years that I strongly believe I could have benefited from my dad the most. His knowledge and wisdom during this period in my life were so essentially needed that nothing else in the world could have possibly mattered to me back then. A lot of things came to me so fast of which I was unfamiliar with. My voice had changed, my attraction to girls had developed, and the acting out against my mother had kicked in. Times like this were critical for me because, as for many other misfortunate kids in my neighborhood, my life could have easily taken me down another path.

Fortunately, the moment I turned 16, I found my first job working at McDonald's. No longer could I allow my mom to struggle alone with taking care of our family. I figured at least if I could support myself and put money in my mom's pocket, our lives could be a little easier. The downside to my work ethic was that it was actually taking my focus away from school.

It had almost gotten to the point where I had no desire to attend school anymore, and I felt that working to support my family was more important. No matter how hard I tried to step up to fill my dad's shoes, this was unacceptable in my mother's eyes. I owe it all to her for pushing me to complete my high school education. I understood how important it was to her that I receive my diploma, and I made sure that I did not let her down. After all, I owed my mom this much for doing all that she did to raise me.

Not long before high school was over, I had been working at a new job for a while. I worked in an upscale, fine-dining hotel-restaurant. Soon after my family broke apart, when my mom and sister moved to Florida and my brother went his way, I was left sleeping anywhere that I could, including in my first car at times. I noticed that I started going through depression, which resulted in some serious, life-threatening weight gain.

At one point, I was homeless, and a new relationship with my father was underway. He offered his sofa to me for a few months, which I graciously accepted. But it was on that very sofa that I nearly lost my life after having a bad reaction to some weight loss pills I ordered from an infomercial. I was rushed to the hospital by an ambulance. After recovery, the doctor explained how close to death I was and went on to say that what I had done was certainly not worth the risk. It goes to show that even considering what appears to be the easier alternative isn't always the wisest route to take.

Of course, I could have blamed that company for selling me pills that almost led to my death. After all, there's no doubt that some other people wouldn't have addressed the situation in this particular manner. It's common to put the blame on other folks instead of looking within ourselves as the root of the problem. I believe many times we fail to do this as individuals. The truth is, avoiding responsibilities does absolutely nothing to change the outcome of our circumstances, and it certainly grants no magical powers for undoing anything from our past.

As I began to experience more life, I could no longer allow my negligence and insecurities to prevent me from following my heart. So, I found a way to overcome the trials and tribulations and pursued more of my dreams. One of the upsides was the opportunity of co-authoring this book. Some people believe in coincidences, which is okay. I believe that everyone is entitled to their opinions. But personally, I'm a believer of the law of attractions. I believe that the universe responds to the vibrations we put out. For example, the way I attracted my wife is living proof of this.

Years prior to the day that I first laid eyes on Sarah, I faithfully visualized meeting and marrying this special woman one day. I remember after meeting her father on the job, I told him that one day I would marry a lady descending from his country. Mind you, at this point, I still hadn't met his daughter. It wasn't until years later on our wedding day when I realized that she was the one I'd visualized as one day being my bride. As I observed and acknowledged this internally, tears of happiness began to roll down my face. I then gave my vows and said, "I do."

I find more irony in this when I think about how we became good friends not long before I started my initial weight loss journey. I could recall the laughter and mockery in regards to my dreams of beating obesity and making it in *Men's Health* magazine from friends and co-workers, but the one who had my back and shared her words of encouragement was Sarah. It was almost as if God sent her from heaven to me. Now, as a result of the support of my lovely wife and in combination with my practice of the law of attraction, I've scored a full-spread feature in *Men's Health* magazine in summer of 2017.

The moral of my story is that no matter what we've been through or the odds place against us, we still have the power to change the dynamics and make ourselves winners. It's important to take whatever appropriate and necessary steps to regain peace in our lives. For example, in order for me to gain some sense of peace, I needed to humble myself and forgive my father for the wrong that he had done in my life. Doing such things will undoubtedly help clear your conscience, and you'll eventually begin seeing the doors of opportunity open up for you as they did for me.

Allow perseverance to guide you to wherever your heart desires to take you. A negative past doesn't have to result in a negative future. Also, understand that the possibilities are always infinite and the power of the law of attraction will prove it so. Believe in yourself and truly understand the beauty that resides within you. I encourage you to become confident in loving yourself and become one with the universe. Trust me; this will inspire the beauty from within you to truly blossom. As a result, you'll have the greatest impact on the world and leave a legacy that will live on for generations to come.

BIO

Lionell Dixon is an author and motivational speaker from South Jersey. He is the oldest of three children raised by his mother, Caroline. Besides growing up and having to battle tough kids in his neighborhood, he also experienced battles with obesity into his adulthood. Even as the odds were set against him, he focused on investing positive energy, which led him to achieve an inspirational 150-pound weight-loss transformation. To date, his life story has ignited a strong passion for helping others who feel lost and are without hope to come out of the shadows and find enough courage to seek and achieve their dreams. His positive message and success story have had a tremendous impact on thousands of lives across the world.

Since his transformation, he has competed in bodybuilding competitions with the hope of being a positive example to all others aspiring to achieve the body of their dreams. Lionell, also known as Lonnie Fresh, wrote his first book titled *Out of the Shadows* which was released in 2016. He then wrote a cookbook, *The 150 Fresh System.* Lionell believes that one must conquer the mind in order to finally be set free of mental self-enslavement. So far, he has been featured on ABC with Philadelphia's Ali Gorman, in *Real Health* magazine, *Healthy Black Men* online magazine, the *Press of Atlantic City*, *Men's Health* magazine, and in a feature film with *Men's Fitness* magazine in New York City

3

Finding Purpose - A Personal Journal

By Dr. David Yoder

"The two most important days in your life are the day you were born and the day you find out why." - Mark Twain

What is your earliest childhood memory? As an adopted child, I cannot remember anything significant until about the age of three. There must have been subconscious blockage of my separation from my birth mother. I imagine my first feelings as a newborn would have been filled with uncertainty and confusion.

My new parents who adopted me were two very adventurous, outgoing parents who had a child of their own but desired to have another child. I believe my first childhood memory was sitting in the sun outside in nature in Bolivia in South America. A change of events occurred during my dad's career in Bolivia, and my parents ended up rescue-adopting twin babies; their mother had died during labor.

After successful paperwork with the local Bolivian government, we relocated to Detroit, Michigan. This part of my childhood was filled with more mixed emotions. I began to question and wonder why I was adopted. *What events led to me being left by my birth parents?*

Unfortunately, in the 1970's, California had a closed-adoption policy, so no information could be provided that would help an individual relocate or track down their birth parents. Ironically, my twin sisters had all the information they could ever wish for.

One day in elementary school during show-and-tell, I decided to make myself be the "show-and-tell." I was quite surprised to find out that not many children knew what it meant to be adopted; that's when I began to feel uniquely different and isolated in my childhood. My twin sisters would often give me the guilt trip for comparing my birth story to theirs as though I wasn't thankful for what had happened. I soon realized that it would be quite pointless to get my hopes up knowing that I couldn't really fulfill my desires to find out anything more about my birth background and history.

I didn't have many friends growing up in middle school and high school. I was very introverted and different than my other friends. I turned my focus toward becoming a good student.

So, much later in my second year of college, I was offered a full scholarship by the National Institutes of Health (NIH) to go to medical school and do research. I felt as if my prayers had been answered. This was everything I could hope for; the scholarship would take care of my education and my living expenses for the next eight years or more. *A major factor of why I was offered this scholarship was due to the combination of my academic performance and being an Asian minority.*

About a year into the scholarship, I started to ask questions about the philosophy of healing and medicine. I felt there was more than just treating symptoms with medications.

I read a book by Deepak Chopra titled "Quantum Healing" and learned there is an entirely different philosophy of health – a "vitalistic" model compared to the "mechanistic" model, which assumes that we are just a bunch of parts and cells that can be manipulated, treated, or medicated and that there is no spirit or soul that exists inside of us.

For no known reason, this invoked and awoken something deep inside of me that was still searching for answers to why I was born, what my purpose was, and how I could find my birth mother. I decided to give up the full scholarship and pursue an alternative path. All of my family and friends thought I was crazy for giving up such a perfect opportunity; they didn't understand why I had to leave Michigan and go to California and pursue a path that had no certainty.

But what also gave me a redirection was a chiropractor, Dr. Karl Johnson. He was a kind and generous mentor who took me in and shared a different philosophy of health and healing. He also treated some physical ailments I had been suffering with since childhood.

Basically, in about nine months I had better vision. I grew taller, my immune system was stronger, and my chronic neck and shoulder tension were gone – all without any special medications or invasive procedures. The only treatment was a spinal correction. This outcome was confirmation for me, and it also released an inner-energy source that encouraged me to continue on my journey to California.

Before I left, I began reading more self-help books to find out more about how I could awake my intuition and fulfill my desires to find my purpose. One of my first books that inspired me was "Chicken Soup for the Soul." This book was filled with many true-life stories of people who had overcome all odds and found their peace and happiness in life. Another book was "The Celestine Prophecy." What I gained from reading this book was that there are no chance meetings in life, and everything has a purpose. The third book that was instrumental was "Jumping Mouse: A Story About Inner Trust." It was a Native American story to teach the younger generations how to learn to trust others.

Finally, I arrived safely in California on my way to a chiropractic program at a college in the San Francisco Bay Area. I was accepted to the chiropractic program which would take another four years to complete and included a final exam that was broken down into four parts over two years.

In between classes, I would try to find time to search for my birth mom. It was 1998 before the Internet was established and before Google was really known for its search tools. I had no name, phone number, or photograph. The only information I had was that my parents were of Thai descent, in good health, and were very young when they had me. I tried contacting some private investigators, and they said that without any information it would be next to impossible to locate them. Out of desperation, I even tried contacting Oprah Winfrey to see if she could help since I knew she had a soft spot for family reunions.

Time slipped by quickly during college, and I had forgotten about the tips and insights that I learned about in my self-help books. So, I realized it was time to start and put them to the test!

One thing I knew was that my family was from Thailand, but the closest association I could find about Thai people was to hang out and try Thai food at the many local restaurants in the Bay Area. During one meal, I made an astute observation that I rarely ever saw Thai people eating at Thai restaurants. I decided to ask the waitress why that was so? She politely informed me that most Thai people eat food that is much spicier and different than what they serve at local restaurants.

So, I logically asked where I could find authentic Thai food. That eventually led to her telling me that most Thai people practice Buddhism and attend the local Buddhist temples on Sundays. I also learned from her that there was a local Buddhist temple less than a mile from where I was renting a place to stay.

Excited, yet uncertain about what would happen next, I decided to make my way to the Buddhist Thai temple in hopes of meeting somebody who might help me reconnect with my birth mother. As I knocked on the front door of the Buddhist temple, I realized while waiting for the door to open that if they only spoke the Thai language, I would be at a loss since I only knew English.

To my surprise, the young man who answered the door was a tall, Caucasian-looking student who spoke perfect English and invited me inside the temple. (Apparently, the monks decided to take in this young man to help him learn their customs. It was a very rare circumstance that they allowed this to happen.) I was just relieved that he spoke perfect English and introduced me to the head monk, Maha Prassart.

Within a very short moment after sharing the little information I had about my birth story, the monk started to nod his head and said that he knew my birth mother! He had been in the Bay Area since 1969, and since I was born in 1970, he knew the local Thai people at the time of my birth, including my mother. This meeting led to a series of other meetings that brought me to another older Thai woman who had my mother's photograph and address in Bangkok, Thailand. When she handed me my mother's address, she said that I could not contact her because she didn't know if my mother ever told anybody about my birth since it was a very secret situation.

Come to find out, my birth mother was not supposed to get pregnant and leave college. Her family would be very upset at her actions. No one else knew about my birth. I was close to reuniting with her, but I felt confused about taking the next step hoping to make it a favorable outcome. I decided to head back to the Buddhist Thai temple to learn the culture and use meditation as a doorway into their world. If one has ever tried meditation, it is truly a very difficult task to learn to quiet the mind. I knew somehow that if I could clear my thoughts and find a clear, peaceful state of mind, God might give me a way to contact with my birth mother.

After dedicating a few months of learning how to meditate after class during sunset meditation, I achieved my goal. Usually, the meditation will proceed as follows: The monks would chant for about thirty minutes, followed by thirty more minutes of silent meditation. It would end by seven o'clock. I would return home and get ready for the next day of school.

On this one special meditation, when I opened my eyes and looked at my watch, it was past 9 p.m.! During my meditation, I traveled out of my body across the ocean toward my birth mom and let her know that I was trying to contact her but wanted to let her know that I had no anger or guilt and was just trying to reconnect and start a new beginning. I felt as if she had seen me and listened to my request and was open to beginning a new relationship.

I took pen to paper and wrote an old-fashioned letter and sent it to the address given to me. It stated that my name is David Yoder, and I was born September 9, 1970, in Berkeley. California, and was in California attending chiropractic college. I wrote that I was hoping to connect with my birth family and that I was told some Thai people at the Thai Buddhist monastery knew of other people who might still be in the area who could help me reconnect. I told her that her name and address were given to me as one of the people who might know about my story. I asked her if she knew about my story, and if she did, could she kindly write back to me and provide any information that could help me reconnect with my birth mother; so basically, I left it up to her at this point to make a decision.

It takes about a week for a letter to arrive in Thailand through regular mail, and a week later, I received a letter from the address provided. In the first sentence, it read, "Dear David… From the information you have provided, I am your birth mother." I instantly knew that my wish had been fulfilled and a piece of my heart was healed that was once lost.

I felt powerful that I somehow had manifested this outcome, and I decided it was also time to meet my future soulmate. During a meditative walk on the beach, I decided to ask God if he could bring me a special person to share my life with. Within that same month, I ended up meeting my future wife.

After graduation, we moved to San Diego and started our family. My wife gave birth to our son Noah on April 12, 2007. He is now ten years old. Last year, I asked Noah if he remembers his birth. He said that he remembered. So, I challenged him and asked him to describe what he saw and felt. He described being inside his mother's body floating around and that he saw the colors red and orange and heard her heartbeat. Then during the excitement of being pushed out during labor, he said he saw me first when he opened his eyes; he said I looked blurry.

Noah did not know yet from science and biology that a newborn's vision is blurry for about a week. From these details, I feel that my son has a distinct memory of his birth moment where I did not. Noah's birth was my life "coming full circle" and realizing that my new purpose had been found!

That purpose is to be the best father and husband and healer that I can be to my family and my community.

Thank you for reading with your eyes and listening with your heart to my story. I hope this awakens something in you and inspires some hope for your story.

....

BIO

Dr. David Yoder discovered throughout his education that he wanted to be a doctor to help those in need. Yoder began a pre-medical course of study. He was granted a full scholarship by the NIH at Wayne State University in Detroit, Michigan, to pursue a special M.D.-Ph.D. program. Going through this program, Yoder soon realized that his analytical brain was being stimulated, but his heart was not into it. He needed to find a different philosophy that incorporated natural healing principles.

On a summer break, Yoder interned with a chiropractor who mentored him on how the mind-body connection worked through the human nervous system. As he became a patient and learned this firsthand, he soon noticed how much healthier his own body became as a result of treatment. But what was more important was the concept that the body can heal itself and that Western medicine was really designed for crisis care and not "health care." With that in mind, Yoder began to pursue a Doctor of Chiropractic degree. And upon graduating from Life Chiropractic College West in the San Francisco Bay Area, he moved to San Diego with his family.

Yoder invites you to begin your journey back to health with the David Yoder Wellness Center. At our wellness center, we will help you by balancing your nervous system with gentle adjustments, energy balancing (B.E.S.T.), proper nutrition, and diet recommendations.

4

The One Truth about Regret and Commitment

By Evan Shellshear

It was a warm summer evening, like most Brisbane days, and I had just left my mother weeping in the departure hall. I boarded my one-way flight to Germany. As I stepped onto that plane I had deliberately put aside thoughts about the consequences of my actions. I'd learned that sometimes it's better that way. I was determined not to let any fears or doubts mutate into insurmountable obstacles blocking the path to my chosen goal.

I wasn't escaping an unhappy upbringing or anything like that. I was just another globally oriented product of a comfortable Western family: middle-class, suburban life. What I was leaving behind wasn't a past I regretted. It was the fear of regretting my future.

However, it wasn't long before reality caught up with mc. Within six months I had no food, no money, and was trembling on the edge of starvation. The effects of my decision to travel to a country where I knew no one and had only the most rudimentary grasp of the language, had become painfully apparent.

This experience shaped the way I approach my life ever since. When I feel something is important to me, but the path to it isn't clear, I know I need to be prepared to commit to the unknown and stick to my goal despite any difficulties. I don't want to live a life wondering, what if?

And that's why I had to do this.

On Jan. 8, 2005, two days before my 22nd birthday, I boarded that one-way flight to Germany full of anticipation. I was packed to the hilt with everything I imagined I would need to accomplish the seemingly impossible: complete a master's degree and Ph.D. in a record four years at one of the world's premier institutes for game theory, Bielefeld University.

My provisions included a thick down jacket, donned in the middle of an Australian summer in preparation for my arrival in a German winter. I also took a closet full of clothes, which had seemed important but would merely reveal my lack of understanding of European weather. They remained untouched for the next six months and were a constant reminder that I was no longer in my homely comfort zone.

After being rejected for a scholarship, I'd deliberately taken just enough money to survive for six months in order to force myself to find work. I'd backed myself into a corner to make sure that when things got difficult I would have to cope on my own. Why? Because when life becomes overwhelming, it is better to burn that bridge back to safety to make sure the focus remains on moving toward one's goal. Although tough, maybe even foolhardy, I knew this approach gave me the best chance of success – or utter failure.

My New Home

When I landed the next day, my first challenge was simply to figure out how to travel from the Dusseldorf airport to my new home, the town of Bielefeld.

I had no idea how the train system worked, nor how to buy a ticket. Looking like a pack camel and dressed in my oversized jacket, I dragged my two large suitcases around the Dusseldorf airport, roaming forlornly toward the train station. I eventually found a ticket machine and spent the next 15 minutes trying to understand it while discovering the limit of German patience.

Sometime later, I was sitting alone on a train whizzing through the northwest German countryside. It wasn't like the sunny, golden beaches of Australia I knew. The region was flattened during World War II and then rebuilt in the form of a desolate industrial landscape blotched with gray buildings, gray factories and gray rain clouds.

I arrived in Bielefeld and was met by an assistant from my new university who drove me to where I would live for the next four years. I was placed with a lovely elderly couple who lived in a stock standard post-war, three-story, yellow plastered German dwelling.

They were a kindhearted pair in their late 60s and knew what it meant to have children abroad. Helga had even practiced so she could welcome me with an English greeting in her lovely German accent. We joked briefly about the weather and the fact that the first time I left home was to travel 10,000 miles to the other side of the world on my own. They pointed out where everything was and told me not to hesitate to ask if I needed anything. I then climbed three narrow flights of stairs, ducking on the final turn to enter the small attic that I would call home.

I unloaded 40 kg (88 pounds) of travel weight and years of preconceptions as I absorbed my surroundings.

It was a cramped space under a sloped, brown, exposed wooden slat roof. The accommodation consisted of three small rooms whose most notable feature was the musty smell of aged abandonment. There was a tiny kitchen with a miniature fridge the size of two beer crates in the corner. Next to it was a small oven and stove, also the size of the fridge, under a skylight window in the slanted roof. The room beside the kitchen was an even smaller bathroom. The final room, my bedroom, would serve as my new headquarters: study, rest and contemplation. Instead of a wall, it had a large window looking out into the fog-hidden hills behind the house. After the short tour, I began unpacking my bags in preparation for the journey ahead.

The Real Journey Begins

The next day would be representative of my time in Germany – the struggle to establish a meaningful life in a new country. My first hurdle was to find a job and avert impending financial disaster.

This was no easy task. I tried everywhere to find employment opportunities; teaching English, manual labor, and even door-to-door sales. Finally I got a break and was employed as a university tutor. Unfortunately, this first job gave me a false sense of security. I only had work during the first university semester and as it came to a close, I realized that I would not have enough money to bridge the rapidly approaching summer holidays.

In desperation, I signed up as a subject for intrusive psychology experiments to earn extra money. I even tried selling some of my possessions. It was all in vain. Two months into the semester break my bank account flatlined. I was broke. I refused to ask my family for financial help as I believed this would weaken my resolve and grant me a bridge back to safety.

To make the situation worse, due to my misunderstanding of the way the bank system worked, I overdrew my account without knowing it. This, however, allowed me to pay the rent for another month before I had to tell my landlords that I had no money. When they asked if everything was OK, I lied and said it was.

It was not.

To keep fit, I frequented the university's pool. On a weekday afternoon, while putting my togs on to go for a swim, I noticed that my pants were loose. I initially thought I had washed them incorrectly and caused them to stretch. It took another week before other not-so-subtle clues led me to a set of scales and the ensuing shock.

Twenty-two pounds had disappeared from a 6-foot-something man who was already lean. I now weighed less than 160 pounds. My ribs were visible and my hands were bony. I knew I was undernourished, but I hadn't noticed the weight loss, which the undeniable reading on the scales confronted me with.

Everything seemed to be falling apart. In addition to the weight loss, I realized that the first six months of work on my master's thesis had been in vain. The mathematical theory I had tried to create was fundamentally flawed and the whole theoretical edifice I had built crumbled before my eyes. I would have to scrap everything I'd done and start again with a new topic. This meant I had to complete my master's from scratch in half a year or be forced out of Germany.

I felt like a complete failure.

That evening I stood in my attic – broke, starving, alone, and on the edge of ruin. I looked at myself and asked why continue? There was no one to cheer me up and there seemed to be no options left.

In that moment, it would have been easy to capitulate and telephone my family in Australia. However, I believed if I gave up, the agony of regret would be much worse than what I was feeling at that moment. The only choice was to continue. I was on a one-way journey and had committed myself to this goal. So, I asked myself, was this all I had in me?

The Journey Ends

I considered what was possible and decided I had to give it one more shot. Over the next six months I found a new supervisor for my master's thesis and began working on what would become a very successful piece of research. I found a new tutoring position and clawed my way out of debt. I started spending more money on food and avoided all other costs in order to put on weight. Within six months, I'd made it out the other side looking a lot better and was accepted into the Ph.D. program.

And the journey didn't stop there. During the following three years, I met my wonderful wife and completed my Ph.D. We left Germany to begin a rewarding life together in Sweden, which was complemented by the arrival of our three children.

In my moments of despair, I had no way to foresee where my journey would lead me.

I found I did have the inner resources to deal with what I had to face. However, without the initial commitment to fight until the end I would not have discovered this. Maybe buying that one-way ticket to a foreign land was what I needed to keep my commitment in place.

Of course it's not always possible to do this. Although I'm no longer in the situation that I cannot afford a return ticket, how do I make sure I achieve my goals now? A way I have found helpful is to tell everyone I'm serious about doing something. If I want to ensure I reach my goals, I tell my friends, my family, announce my vision to the world, and by doing so I make a powerful commitment. The expectations of the people closest to me can be as effective as a one-way ticket.

By removing that bridge back to safety you can push yourself to reach the far horizons of your aspirations, ambitions and dreams. The one truth about regret and commitment is that you have to commit to not living in fear of regret to discover what life holds in store for you.

....

BIO

Evan Shellshear has lived and learned in Germany, Sweden and Australia. He has an optimistic attitude on life and is grateful for what he has. He is the author of the best selling book on Amazon, ***Innovation Tools,*** and the highly successful game *Bug Rope* on Google Play.

Twitter: @eshellshear
www.facebook.com/innovationtoolsbook;
website: simultek.com.au
Book: http://amzn.com/B01F3NDLP4
evan@simultek.com.au

5

Dinner and a Lesson

By Luis O. Cuebas

Growing up in the 1970s and '80s, we didn't really watch much television. It was reserved for family night. I'm talking about a time when TV both reflected and defined our American culture. From sitcoms to soap operas, game shows to Super Bowl commercials, television was how we learned and observed the times and connected as a nation. When I did ask to watch a little bit of the tube, I was normally given three options – read a book, write a book, or go play in traffic. So I started writing when I was young. As a kid, I wrote poems and creative short stories to pass the time. Several of them were about fantastic characters on faraway islands. A few were even published.

I was born and raised on an island in the Caribbean for the first five years of my life. Spanish is my first language. My brother and I were raised by my genius mom and bonafide national hero dad. Life was pretty much perfect...until we moved away. Our family relocated to Colorado in the fall of 1978 after Dad fell in love with the U.S. Air Force Academy's surrounding area. Colorado Springs and the Front Range became home. My dad served as an overseas secret intelligence officer for the U.S. armed forces. He was very well-decorated and a strict leader for sure, yet he was a blast with a contagious laugh and a quick-wit sense of humor. Dad was a ton of fun, but make no mistake; he was a warrior at heart.

Suppertime was a sacred ritual in our house. Bikes, toys, balls, and tail-ends all in the garage by sunset. Blinds closed and curtains drawn at dusk. Washed up and sitting down for dinner before dark. Telephone off the hook before any meal was plated. No toys, complaining, or excuses allowed at the *Table of Champions*. Some of my dad's most powerful life lessons were delivered at the dinner table. He was great at telling a story. He used clever, concise words to convey deep, powerful ideas to get his message across. He would say plenty with few words. His compelling lessons shared insightful concepts of wisdom for radical self-improvement. Some were stories of triumphant victory over self-doubt and life's seemingly insurmountable obstacles. These lessons also reinforced our family's policies and codes of conduct.

He had a way of positively impacting people with his words. Some people would travel to come to spend a day or an evening and a meal with my dad. Those dinners were often the best. I loved it when we had company over for supper. My parents were the perfect hosts. My brother and I would be on our best behavior. Dinner and a lesson from dad were always prepared with a serving of Dad's genuine compassion, a portion of his unique sense of humor, and a healthy side of cognitive disruption. Every experience was topped off with mom's gracious hospitality and loving support. Dad's lessons would blow your mind. Laughter was always a component to his creative parables. Folks would leave our home finding themselves physically, emotionally, and spiritually refreshed. I saw lives change as a result of these positive interventions and private times shared over an intimate meal. I have learned how words, language, and stories can forever change someone's life.

"Friends are the family you get to choose in life – treat them well, and feed them with all of your love," my dad would say, "For this nourishes your very soul."

Each story and lesson dad shared was crafted with a special message. Sometimes, it was a joke or slant on a colorful metaphor.

Other times he would explore the original, etymological meanings of critical keywords related to a person's life situation. He would always share whatever value he could to help others through his words. He taught me how to be a real, genuine, and transparent man. He showed me how to give hope and inspire others – to identify with an individual's desire to truly change, grow, and improve their life. He taught me to serve others with my whole heart. He knew how important it was that we laugh at ourselves in any given situation and how to properly share humor and joy with food. With time, I began to journal and take down some of the most powerful lessons that really impacted people.

I have come to appreciate and better understand how connection, communion, and community are three essential human elements of life. I call these our three core human realities. These three realities are auto-inspiring, interdependent expressions of our human condition. All are required for a life of abundant fulfillment. Our mind, body, and spirit are all fed and stimulated by these three experiences. For several years now, I have traveled abroad as a journalist for various nonprofits and missions around the world. I employ Dad's techniques to connect with people and learn from them.

"People, not things, should always come first in life, son," Dad would often remind me.

We too often become distracted by our needs, and we lose sight of the beauty of our deeds. Our *humanness* is measured by how we impact and are impacted, by others. The most precious human facets of our existence can be lost when we are otherwise consumed with ego, pursuing status or material possessions. I have learned to be cautious of *needs*. Needs can own you. It's better to f*ocus on life's essentials, your beautiful deeds.* Family, friends, neighbors, coaches, and mentors – their ideas and words can inspire us where motivation doesn't seem to budge us. Previous psychological schools of thought on human motivation provided 5, 6, 7 and 8-stage hierarchy-of-needs models on fulfillment and change through personal growth or "self-actualization." However, our life priorities become dramatically skewed without respecting the three core realities of connection, communion, and community.

'Eudaemonia' is the Greek word for "human flourishing." It means comfort, contentment, happiness, health, prosperity, protection, safety, security, welfare, profit, and success. This one word pretty much covers the full spectrum and hierarchy of human needs. A life-inspired mental framework is the key to human flourishing and preferable over a needs-based mindset.

The three core human realities also correlate with eudaemonia and the 7 Human Essentials for Inspired Life Mastery and Abundance: Accomplishment, Certainty, Significance, Connection, Growth, Contribution, and Variety. A fully realized inner-self has the power to harness all seven human essentials, generate compounding enthusiasm, and provide the required inspiration to master any task and conquer every life challenge. An individual with a completely realized inner-self, or self-actualization, can become virtually unstoppable when connected to a supportive community. The results are breathtaking to witness, like the beauty of a butterfly shedding its cocoon and drying its wings to fly for the first time.

Words, love, and ideas ~ what we leave behind.

There is something compelling about triumphant human victory over self-doubt and seemingly insurmountable obstacles. I find inspiration in seeing and hearing of others who are overcoming life's challenges in spite of pain and adversity. Words, language, and stories have always fascinated me. Sharing a meal and hearing others share their stories and dreams is the best way to spend any evening. These moments of beautiful human interaction cause me to write and study.

My father's work has recently become my own. I have learned to master my own personal creative process for a life of freedom, abundance, and fulfillment and now teach this system and framework to others. Most of the interactive workshops and creative breakthrough sessions I facilitate today are shared over a meal and include a form or creative art and/or music in the experience. It's my passion and creative destiny. My vision is to share Dad's work with individuals, groups, and audiences around the world – one dinner, one lesson, and one story at a time. Sharing these valuable secrets to a successful and abundant life is my mission – to inspire and improve lives through good ideas and creative connections.

My desire is that people find inspiration, freedom, abundance, and true fulfillment in life as we discover our own special way of inspiring, sharing, and connecting with others around us. One of my favorite lessons from my dad is, "Our love, talents, and time are the only real gifts we have to offer the world. We can't take them with us when we go." I have learned this lesson well in life.

A lesson of my own I now share with others comes from this understanding: *Our words, love, and ideas are what we leave behind, defining our lasting human value.*

....

BIO

I moved from Colorado to Nashville, Tennessee, in 2008 to pursue my dream of being a successful entrepreneur, author, and public speaker. It took two years to become certified as a performance consultant, and I went on to earn master neurolinguistics and NLP training certifications. Mom and Dad moved to Nashville in

2010. Dad had become ill and wanted to be near his sons and grandchildren before he died – what a life lesson itself. Dad passed away November 21, 2011. There are no words to capture how I value the last year we spent together. I miss his voice, his eyes, and his ever-timely lessons. "Give time to time," Dad would often say – so true. I had the honor to catch up on many sunset sermonettes and dinner lessons with my dad before he left us for the last time that Thanksgiving.

As a professional, I have worked for some of the world's largest organizations as an executive brand strategist, director of communications, corporate learning technologist, studio director, producer, and U.S. government information specialist with a top-secret information clearance. As an entrepreneur, I've owned several businesses, including automotive service stations, investment properties, and a successful digital marketing agency for independent artists and creative entrepreneurs. For my community, I serve on the YMCA board and help raise funds for nonprofits and missions around the world. As a father, I prioritize my family and carry on my dad's legacy to impact and positively influence future generations. As a man, I focus on a healthy balance between faith, family, and freedom – life's truest riches.

As a writer, author, and journalist, I'm still a creative entrepreneur at heart. I'm always working on an artistic project, or three. I enjoy time with authentic people, the outdoors, live music, traveling, and experiencing new things with new friends. I love to spend the rest of my time at home, cooking, writing, reading, playing music, relaxing, and creating memories with loved ones.

Luis O. Cuebas
PO Box 3292
Brentwood, TN
37204-3292

20 BEAUTIFUL MEN

www.omarcuebas.com
luisocuebas@gmail.com
www.facebook.com/t.omar.cuebas
www.instagram.com/omarcuebas/
www.twitter.com/OmarCuebas
www.linkedin.com/in/luis-omar-cuebas-895bb91b/
www.youtube.com/channel/UCH6N0CgJv9L_DcB5fa7dpBA

6

Search For Harmony

By Ian Hawkins

"You know that money you owe me?"
"Yeah."
"Don't worry about paying it back."

Those words shattered my heart in an instant, and I said nothing for what seemed an eternity. We both knew what it meant; I just had no idea how to respond. That was my dad's way of communicating to me that he was going to die ... soon.

As I looked back, I realized I had never felt truly connected to my Dad, who I idolized. A combination of factors meant that despite all the love that he offered to me and my siblings, I struggled to connect with him in a way that I craved, and this hurt.

He was painfully quiet at times, and as an introvert, I know he must have been exhausted by the time he came home from his job as a math teacher. He often collapsed on the couch after work and fell asleep. It is no coincidence that some of my fondest childhood memories are from school holidays when he was able to dedicate so much time to us without distraction or frustration.

He was certainly not lazy as he spent most nights dedicating his time to various school and church- related groups and activities. This was a great source of frustration to me as he seemed to give so much in so many areas of his life, yet I felt like I was way down the list of priorities. As a highly sensitive child, I wanted a deeper connection with him, yet my own shyness and lack of confidence held me back. As I got older, I wanted to talk with him more, but we had little in common to discuss. The way I look at it now, this was no one's fault. The reality was that we had different personalities, and neither of us had the skills to bridge the gap.

I believe we do the best job we can as a parent with the skills that we have. Growing up in Branxton, a tough, no-nonsense, coal mining town 200km (120 miles) north of Sydney, Australia, would have involved some fairly harsh moments in Dad's upbringing. Given this, I am extremely grateful for the fact that, as my sister said to me recently, he had the strength to give us a vastly toned down version of what he would have experienced as a child. Despite his own pain, he showed us so much kindness and love. Toned down though it may have been, we still experienced moments where Dad's frustration spilled over and the tone of his words hurt. I didn't understand at the time, but I often made mistakes just to draw some attention from him. This must have been as frustrating and hurtful to him as it was for me.

Many years later I realized history was repeating itself, and my children were becoming just like me.

Misplaced Trust

My childhood was mostly a happy time with lots of fun family times playing with my siblings. I am extremely grateful for all the support my family gave me. For example, Dad was a man of action. In an era that it was not the thing to do, he helped with housework and in all facets of raising five children. Mum taught me all about empathy and seeing the world from others' perspective. I have particularly fond memories of chatting with her each afternoon in the kitchen and getting stuff off my chest. But at the same time, I dealt with a lot of personal pain as well.

As a shy and highly sensitive youngster, I spent a lot of time quietly observing, wondering how people could be so unkind to each other. So I made a conscious decision as a 6- year- old to help people who needed love, compassion, and connection, while most of the world was giving each other pain.

As the years passed, this urge never left, but it also never developed. If anything, it slowly eroded as my mistrust grew and my self-confidence took hit after hit. My life became one of contradictions. I craved connection, and I longed to fit in, but at the same time lacked the confidence to do anything about it and shied away from people. I was trying to keep everyone happy on one hand, and on the other, I dealt with my poor self-worth by cutting down and hurting those closest to me to make myself feel better.

As the middle child I had that "poor me" attitude, often feeling "the odd man out," too young for the cool stuff my older brother and sister were doing and too old for the fun things my younger brothers were doing. This neglected middle-child complex impacted other areas too. Like all siblings, we fought, often over petty things. And to me, it felt like more often than not I would be the person that wore the blame. This continued until I hit about 13, and I can still remember the day that I decided I would no longer fight that. I would just accept whatever came my way from my parents and just wear it. I gave up so much power that day. The power to be strong and to stand up for myself and for what I believed was the truth.

That power is something that I have only been able to rediscover in the last couple of years. But in my teen years, I never felt good enough. I felt judged; I constantly worried about what others thought of my actions and whether I was upsetting people. I made decisions based on what others would think of me and not what I really wanted.

The one place I thrived and had a reasonable level of self-confidence, courage, determination, and drive was on the sporting field. At the age of 17, alcohol provided another welcomed boost to my self-confidence and soon become a crutch that I relied on in social settings. At the same time, it sapped my energy and stifled my motivation. Thankfully for me, there was one defining moment during this period when I took a risk that was completely out of character and way out of my comfort zone. I knew I had to follow my heart, so I summoned the courage to pick up the phone and call the girl who would later become my wife. Socially, we were having a ball, but my career suffered as I drifted through my 20's with no direction and nothing inspiring me to be better.

In my 30's, there were three major catalysts for me to make big changes in my life. My wife and I had our first child in 2004, and from that moment, I realized that I wanted to provide as much as possible to give our daughter the best possible chance in life. This desire only grew with the birth of our son in 2007.

There Has To Be More To Life

Then my Dad died in 2005, *and I learned nothing makes you question your existence like losing someone you love.* But, I still didn't know how to change. I just knew that I wanted my life to be different, that I wanted to be better.

I can remember being at work a few years later and thinking, *I keep kidding myself thinking I am happy, but am I really?* I knew I wasn't. At this point, I was hungry for change, but I felt trapped and wasn't sure how to change. I didn't know where to start, so I didn't.

It was the final of these catalysts that actually triggered me to take significant action. In 2011, a random conversation (or so it seemed at the time) with my sister-in-law changed everything. Her dad had planned to retire but was still working as his superannuation (*superannuation* refers to regular payment made to a fund by an employee toward a future pension) had crashed in the GFC (global financial crisis). This made no sense to me. *How could it be that you could work all your life and then be at the mercy of the financial markets come retirement age?* That day, I became determined to take control of my life and provide financial security for my family.

I started searching for answers to my financial future, and soon after, my brother sent me an email that would change my life forever. From the email, I signed up to a wealth building website that was all about shifting your mindset. I downloaded all the free audio and started listening to it every day. Although there were days that I cringed and couldn't face listening too much, I was also fascinated. Most days I would listen to it for at least 30 minutes. I went to the one-day workshop linked to this site, and I signed up for the mentoring program.

Michael, my first real mentor, asked me, "Why do you want to sign up to my mentorship program?" Without hesitation, I answered, "Because I am sick of mediocrity!" And so my personal development journey started and soon accelerated. I said goodbye to my old life and started building a life where I was happy being me. I was only 38; it wasn't too late.

While I was upgrading my financial mindset, I was making shifts in other parts of my life at the same time. Suddenly I was being exposed to new high-performance principles daily, most of them so simple yet so powerful. I started recording my progress and frustrations in a daily journal. I began to shift from blaming to taking personal responsibility. I started reading books again. I learned that *when the student is ready, the teacher will appear,* and this became a theme for my life as a new teacher, mentor, coach, motivator, or healer appeared at just the right moment.

For instance, I wanted to become a calm, patient, and happy dad instead of snapping at my wife and kids and then beating myself up internally afterwards. I was so focused on blaming the negatives in my life that I was neglecting all that was good. If I instead concentrated on all the positives I had learned (particularly from my mum and dad) and expressed gratitude for those, more solutions would find me, and I would have started to heal my internal pain – solutions like the book I randomly found for $1 at a second hand book sale in a golf club bar of all places, which introduced me to meditation, a practice that has brought me a calm and focus I didn't think was possible. While I am by no means perfect, I have improved dramatically in this area of my life.

I'd shifted from years of drifting and playing small and uncomfortable with success to rapid growth and regular pushes out of my comfort zone. At times, it felt like I was accelerating out of control. Much of this new-found confidence came when I was introduced to a tool that helped me see how I could drastically improve my life by focusing on my natural strengths.

This was a game-changer as I came to understand why I had been so easily distracted throughout my life, why detailed work exhausted me even though my attention to detail was strong, how trusting my instincts helped me to succeed, and why nothing in my life gave me a bigger buzz than connecting with people to help them. Once I'd taken the training to be a consultant, I used those tools to help my family, staff, and friends find the same "flow" in their own life. Once I better understood the people I was spending most of my time with, my ability to communicate, my leadership skills, and my relationships thrived. I soon realized that I shouldn't hold back because someone seemed intimidating, or because I felt that they were "out of my league." I was playing a much bigger game becoming comfortable with my success. And even though it was scary at times, I was absolutely loving it!

One of my natural gifts is that when I learn something, I immediately think of someone else it will help, and this happened continually through my first years of rapid change. At times, I tried to force things and would hit resistance. Eventually, I came to the realization that I needed to make changes myself, set a positive example, and let those who are interested either come along for the ride or ask for help. When my personal development steered me toward building a movement, I decided that I wanted to help other dads make positive change.

Being a dad is the toughest job I have ever done, and there are times when you feel like you spend all your time satisfying everyone else's needs but never your own. If you have ever felt like this and asked yourself — "Is there more to life than this," the answer is a resounding *YES*. When you find the direction that is right for you, build the vision, and commit to taking action, you will start to get excited and watch your life change. If you believe it, you *are* capable of so much more. When you break free from the limiting beliefs that are holding you back, you will own your success.

When you dream big, take big action and know that the universe is conspiring to help you, life starts to get exciting. You realize that the answer to all of life's problems are there for you to find if only you will look.

Over the past five years, my new thirst for personal development has helped me to find inspiration, motivation, and direction in my life. I have learned how to find my unique path to high energy, optimum health, life harmony, financial security, a life to get excited about, and how to help other dads to do the same.

Living With Purpose

You CAN do anything you REALLY want in this life.

I didn't understand this statement until recently, so I asked myself, "W*hat do I really want?"* Deep down did I want to play sports for my country, go to the Olympics or be a famous musician? No. From all I experienced, I learned all I have ever really wanted in life is to help everyone around me to be kind to each other and to live in harmony.

BIO

Ian's movement mission is to inspire 100,000 people all over the world to discover direction, confidence, accelerated growth and re-connection so they can live a life that until now they have only dreamed about. A person who is being the best version of them-selves becomes inspired to create a life of harmony. This harmony ripples into every part of their life – their family, friends, workplace, community, and their entire world. His mission is to bring harmony to the world one person at a time.

inspireddads.com
facebook.com/inspireddads
facebook.com/groups/inspireddadshealthdirectionpurpose
twitter.com/inspireddads
linkedin.com/in/ianhawkinsinspireddads

7

Pivot

By Evan Rose

By all accounts, it was a normal day. I woke up at my normal time. Got dressed in my usual jeans, a button-down shirt, and loafers. I said goodbye to my now wife, then girlfriend, and left our apartment in Morningside Heights in Manhattan for the 1 Train. The rest of my commute went along seamlessly. Before long, I arrived at my office where I was helping to build a large web application. I got my morning fix of coffee and sat down to go through the emails from the previous day.

I was just about ready to break open my code editor and start knocking out tasks when I got a call from my Mom. *A call from Mom at 10:30 a.m. on a Tuesday? She could be calling just to say hi, but something felt off.* I answered and heard a deafening silence. What followed were two words that would change my life forever. "He's gone."

My mind went into a panic. The best I could come up with was "Nah, no he's not." She responded as calmly as a mother could, "He's gone, baby. Come home."

My brother had leaped to his death from a 13-story building while I was drinking terrible office coffee and leisurely checking my emails. It felt like my world had been shifted 180 degrees, and my feet felt like hands. I rushed to my supervisor and told him what happened. He understood immediately and agreed to inform my team. I quickly gathered my things and got to the elevator lobby before collapsing.

For those of you reading who have lost someone close to you, you can probably recall the wrenching pain of the loss. For those of you who haven't, I hope that you never have to, but the feeling is like having someone reach into your midsection and grab a handful of your organs. It truly is emotional pain manifested as debilitating, physical pain.

I rode up town in a cab. The driver wasn't sure what to make of a 6-foot-2 grown man crying in the back of his car, but he was kind enough not to inquire. As we passed blocks I've seen hundreds of times, I felt like I was viewing the world from behind a stained-glass window. Everyone's lives were continuing as if mine wasn't destroyed. It was utterly isolating. It dawned on me that this was really happening. I was going through one of those moments in life that you pass through but can never come back from. We stopped at my apartment to pick up my girlfriend before going to my childhood home in Westchester. As we drove up to Westchester, I was silent, but her presence made the situation bearable despite the wave of emotions that crashed every few minutes.

The next couple of days were a whirlwind of family visits, memories of my brother Steve, and reflection. Having family around helped, but the most important thing I learned was that I was in control of my state of mind. The loss of a loved one can be an all-consuming void if you let it. There are dark paths, and there are light paths. Succumbing to self-defeating thoughts like "Why didn't I stop this?" or "I should have done more!" anchor you in a past you cannot change. This can only lead you to more thoughts of regret that are self-perpetuating.

The biggest trap I fell into along the way was thinking of my loss as the main loss. When I framed my thinking from the perspective of my own loss, I couldn't help but spiral into thoughts of a future that had been stolen from me – an inherently negative outlook. It was when I shifted my thinking to what the world had lost without him that I had an epiphany. The epiphany was that nothing ever truly dies. He would live on intangibly through the memories he left others with and tangibly through the impact he had on his friends and loved ones. In remembering him and honoring him, his loved ones and the actions he inspired in us would be his legacy.

So, I got to thinking. *How would Steve be remembered?* If people only went by the press, he would be a statistic. The suicide of another Black male would pass by without any action taken to stop the trend. So, I set out to tell not only his story but the story of our family and others dealing with mental illness.

The story started out as a simple Tumblr post. I expected it might reach my network and from that group perhaps someone would be dealing with something similar and be comforted by our experience. It wound up reaching tens of thousands of people. Soon after, I started getting messages from dozens of friends, colleagues, and complete strangers. What shocked me is that these weren't just "I'm sorry for your loss" messages. People were reaching out to share their own struggle, their brother's, sister's, parent's and children's struggles with mental illness. They were saying that they felt empowered by what I had shared, to not only share with me but that it also made them feel more comfortable in their own situations. It warmed my heart and gave me a sense of purpose to know that my family's suffering wouldn't be in vain. I knew what we needed to do.

The next day, I called a family meeting. In attendance were three generations, all saddled with the grief of loss. I tossed out the idea that we should form a foundation with a core goal being that no family ever again has to go through what we were going through, and if they did, there would be resources and support available for them. We got out a seemingly endless supply of Post-it notes and wall-sized drawing boards and got to work. The idea that began that day grew into a foundation, which is today called The Steve Fund. It has brought together clinicians, higher education professionals, students, and families to address the unique mental health issues that people of color face during their college years where these problems are highly likely to manifest.

What we've learned over the years is that mental health issues are more insidious than many of the common illnesses. The array of mental health issues you can have is wide, and the medicine available is ham-handed for many. On top of that, mental health issues come with nasty stigmas attached.

When you break your arm, you don't feel bad about getting a cast. However, when you are feeling less than yourself, many are afraid to seek help. The stigma is often strongest in minority communities where the pressure is high to be strong or unbreakable. The truth is that we all need help at one time or another. A better way to think about mental health is a continuum rather than good or bad, broken or fixed. Think of it as a sliding scale where you might fall differently on different days. The continuum approach opens the door for everyone to engage in much-needed self-care. It also opens the door for dialogue, not only with professionals but with peers as well. Communities that can connect can help each other heal.

From this great tragedy, the Steve Fund grew and became an incredibly meaningful part of my and my family's life, but that wasn't the only hidden blessing Steve gave. During the same period in my life, I was trying to figure out what my purpose was. I knew that my passion was to create using technology, but I wasn't sure what exactly to create. In the wake of Steve's passing, I saw a path forward. I would take aspects of his personality and merge them into my own so that I would live for both of us. His analytical nature, attention to detail, and compassion for others became my own, and they helped me develop the confidence I needed to launch my firm, Rose Digital.

As with any new firm, there were countless late nights, setbacks, and uncertainty. Every setback I faced, I surmounted with a drive that emanated from my new charge, to live for him and myself in a way that honored us both. What started as a small software development shop consisting of me, myself, and I became a 28-person outfit doing work for Fortune 500 clients and agencies. In the same period, the Steve Fund went from a few aggrieved family members in a room to hundreds of clinicians, college officials, mental health advocates, and allies in rooms at Brown, Stanford, and Washington University in St Louis.

I thank God and Steve every day that despite the tragedy that befell our family, I am able to work with incredible people daily on multiple fronts in my life. The greatest tragedy that has ever happened to me became one of my greatest blessings.

....

BIO

Evan Rose is a web/mobile applications developer and entrepreneur. In 2014, he started Rose Digital – a New York-based, minority-owned digital agency. Since then, he has built and delivered web and mobile applications for companies like Ford, American Express, and Zoetis. Evan is also a co-founder and president of The Steve Fund, the nation's only organization focused on supporting the mental health and emotional well-being of college students of color.

(914) 715 9980
evan@rosedigital.co
www.twitter.com/evanmrose
www.rosedigital.co
www.stevefund.org

8

The Rocking Chair

By David James Rodriguez

I was born and raised in a small town in Northern California. After being a paperboy, a pizza-maker, a grocery clerk, a burger-flipper, a restaurant waiter, and a fitness counselor, I began my first business.

That business flopped. So I started a few more, and those failed too. Then at age 23, I met my first mentor, who owned an insurance agency, and he helped me build a business, which I sold at age 26. This allowed me to move to South Korea where I taught English for about a year at a high-performance school and college.

My time abroad allowed me a break from the hustle of the insurance business so that I could focus on my inner life, such as the development of my philosophy, beliefs, and purpose in life. While there, I heard of the "Rocking Chair Principle":

> *Imagine that you, dear reader, are now 100 years old. You are sitting in a rocking chair on your front porch. You rock the chair back and forth. Back and forth, again. You grasp the arms of the rocking chair with both hands as you remember and reflect upon your successful life. You smile. You show your teeth as you grin with total self-satisfaction. You put your hands in the air, arms outstretched, and say to yourself, "I did it. Yes, I lived my life on my terms. I lived my dreams. I am so grateful. I am blessed and happy."*

So now you may wonder, w*hat is 'It'? What is my dream? What are we talking about here?*

We are talking about life.

We are talking about the conversation every mature person eventually has with themselves.

Do you know what your purpose in life is? Have you identified your dreams?

At age 29, I sure didn't. And despite being in a formal schooling environment for 17 years, nobody asked me what my dreams were. When I asked myself this question initially, I thought I'd like to earn a lot of money and enjoy my wealth sitting on the best beaches on Earth. Perhaps I'd find a wife and start a family. That seemed sufficient at the time, given my level of consciousness. However, as I started to think about life, death, and my *Rocking Chair*, I felt a deep desire to live a meaningful life that would make this world better for future generations. Somewhere I read the quote: "We don't inherit the earth from our parents; we borrow it from our children."

I thought, *Yeah! I will soon be in my Rocking Chair, and my kids will continue this cycle of life. So, besides money, what else could I give them?*

I didn't know how I could make a difference. I didn't know what I should do, or even what I wanted to do.

During my early business ventures, a mentor named Arthur L. Williams was introduced to me through his books and videos. He was a high school football coach turned successful businessman who was passionate and authentic. He said, "I'm not selling a product. I'm correcting an injustice."

Then the great artist Roberto Benigni said to me, "Identifying and fighting evil is the start of every happiness."

And another teacher taught me, "You will find your purpose when you identify what was missing from your childhood and work to bring that to the world."

As I combined these ideas with my personal experiences, it was beginning to become clear that what was knocking on my heart, and stirring up my strongest emotions, was the time I spent from age 6 to 23 in a formal schooling environment.

I spent many years in those school buildings, but I found greater inspiration and knowledge from outside sources like books, events, and informal teachers. The lessons and real-world success strategies learned from my informal educational experiences were never addressed during the 17 years of my formal education. On many occasions, I often asked myself, "Why didn't anyone teach me this in school?"

Did you ever ask yourself this question?

In general, my formal teachers and professors were all nice people, but most were uninspiring to me, and only one left a lasting impression.

So why was this important information about success, happiness, and purpose omitted from my educational experience?

When I dug into the subject further, seeking answers to this question, I discovered an incredible amount of data that documented the original intentions of the public-school system. And, specifically, I identified a serious glitch in the school system – the policy of *mandatory attendance.*

It took me years to understand the importance of this discovery. But once it came, I knew I had found the injustice and evil that I was going to invest my life trying to correct.

The key fact that rocked my world is that the government monopoly mandatory attendance schools were designed to create obedient citizens and consumers for the benefit of the state and large corporations.

So, what was my plan to correct this injustice?

For years I didn't know. I kept reading and thinking. I researched and sought out new teachers. During this period, I was paying attention to politics. In fact, I started pursuing a political solution to the problem of mandatory attendance schooling. However, it turns out that there is a lot of money in the school business through contracts with book publishers, builders, food-makers, suppliers, unions, and other special interests. These groups are quite pleased with the current school system, despite its failings, and intend on maintaining the status quo.

I read books from as far back as the 1930's and 1960's that were expressing similar opinions and criticisms that I had, yet the school system had not improved. Actually, it got worse, and today many high school graduates are barely literate. Some graduates can't read at all after 12 years of mandatory schooling.

In my search for genuine, revolutionary solutions, I came across the words of R. Buckminster Fuller who wrote, "You never change things by fighting the existing reality. To change something, build a new model that makes the existing model obsolete."

That was it! I had found that wise phrase just before I lost hope that I would ever find a meaningful solution to the mandatory school system. It was clear to me that if I was truly going to change the system, I was going to have to build something better than the existing school model.

But how was I going to do that?

Again, I was clueless. However, it was obvious that I would have to start my own school and show the world that there is a better way to learn than mandating attendance at school and making students follow a curriculum that is impersonal and irrelevant to their lives.

In my research, I came across an organization, the Alternative Education Resource Organization (AERO). I looked further into its decades of work and was pleasantly surprised to see it had something I wanted. It was an online course called "How to Start a School."

I took AERO's four-month course, and to my great delight, it introduced me to a school called Summerhill, founded in the Unit ed Kingdom by A.S. Neill, which allows students to attend class on a voluntary basis. The classes are 100% optional, not mandatory. It has been a successful school for over ninety years. (Search YouTube: "Summerhill 2008")

This course helped me see an entirely new possibility for empowered learning. Realizing that I was still rather ignorant about schools that gave students the freedom to pick their classes and design their own lives, I wanted to learn more. That's when I created my own live events called the Education Options Expo in California where I'd bring like-minded educational entrepreneurs and promote their schools to parents as I discovered the details of their successful programs. After four events, and hundreds of lives being positively affected, I knew it was time for my own school, Valor Academy, to begin moving forward.

On a visit to New York for an AERO conference, I came up with a strange idea to reach out to one of my heroes, John Taylor Gatto – the former two-time State Teacher of the Year and prolific author who wrote *The Underground History of American Education*, among other great books. I decided to contact him because he is a legend among respectful learning communities, but many parents have yet to discover him. However, these same parents have heard of Horace Mann, who was the key man responsible for enacting mandatory attendance policies for schools in Massachusetts in 1852 and used the state as the bully enforcer for any parent who dared to disobey the new attendance laws.

This angers me because it violates the natural human rights every person has to choose where they learn and spend their time.

I figured if I got permission from Mr. Gatto to use his name on a future project, it would be one way to apply Fuller's idea to make the existing model of schooling obsolete because his writings are incredibly empowering. Once parents understand the severe immorality of being forced to put their kids into certain buildings for twelve years, they may look for educational options that respect their child.

During my visit with Mr. Gatto, he approved my idea and then gave me an invitation. He asked me to re-publish his life's work, *The Underground History of American Education*, which had been out of print for nearly a decade.

Having no previous experience in book publishing, but wanting to empower parents and students around the globe, I said, "Yes!" And as it turned out, many prominent thought leaders such as Robert Kiyosaki, Daniel Pink, and Christiane Northrup were also big fans of Gatto and had endorsed his writings.

As I continued to dig into solutions for mandatory attendance schooling, I found other courageous leaders who had decided to grow their own learning programs. People like Wes Beach, Pat Farenga, Grace Llewellyn, Daniel Greenberg, Kenneth Danford, and Dayna Martin have departed entirely from the mandatory school system and have helped thousands of students find their passions and begin creating lives they love.

Like the bold leaders of mankind's history, these people, and many others stood up for what they believed to be right. They broke away from the crowds and left the bullying state in the dust. There isn't a good reason why parents need permission to educate their own kids. Parents are a child's primary teachers and instructors for life.

The solution that gives children around the world the best chance to experience more freedom and joy than their parents, in my opinion, is to allow them to choose their own studies. They become more fulfilled. They escape the immoral system of schooling that disrespects their free will while the state loses the control it has over our lives.

For now, I leave you to make mandatory attendance schools obsolete. There is a better way to learn. The existing model of schooling is unacceptable. This is the injustice I'm working to correct that will make me look back in my *Rocking Chair* and be proud.

I hope you will make some time today to find your "It" from your *Rocking Chair.* If you find it and pursue it, I believe you will have an amazing life of freedom and joy. Do it right now. Your future self will thank you.

....

BIO

David James Rodriguez is the publisher of *The Underground History of American Education* by the world-renowned schoolteacher, John Taylor Gatto. He is also the founder of the Education Options Expo, which is an event where parents are introduced to respectful schools and approaches to learning and hear from world leaders who are working on future models of education today.

Mr. Rodriguez was born and raised in California, where he attended public school. He received a business degree from San Jose State University. His newest book project with Mr. Gatto has exclusive contributions from Dr. Ron Paul, G. Edward Griffin, and Lew Rockwell and will be made into a film in 2019.

Mr. Rodriguez is the founding principal of Valor Academy – a private school that empowers students to pursue their own interests, passions, and dreams assisted by courses he's created at HomeschoolLeader.com. Both companies help students escape disrespectful schools immediately.

He is also the author of the upcoming book *The Apprenticeship: An Empowered Model of Learning that Respects Students, Parents, and Teachers While Costing Almost No Money.*

HomeschoolLeader.com – Valor-Academy.com
IG: Homeschoolleader – Twitter: @djrodriguez2105

9

The Director of My Movie

By Carlos D. Campbell Jr.

Ten years have passed, and I think back to that day when my life seemed to be over – when my bad behavior had finally *paid off*. It was rather ironic, but it was then when I started to search for the true purpose of my life. It was not the best way, but sometimes it takes for us to fall before we learn how to truly walk.

I was the architect of my life, but I did not have the slightest idea. I was the director of my movie, but the role I was playing at the beginning of my movie was one of a villain, a selfish and self-destructive man finding reasons to end it all at any cost.

Because of my life experiences, no dad around, and leaving my mother at the age of 14 to move to the U.S., I had to adapt the only way I knew how. My mother decided to send me to live with my grandmother in San Diego because dozens of my childhood friends were being lost and often killed by gang violence in my hometown of Panama. But arriving in a new country was a culture shock, and it seemed that everyone was against me. I trained myself not to love or open myself to anyone. This method helped me cope better with life. I had also learned to run away from everyone and everything. And because I had so much anger built in, it was easy for anyone to start a fight with me just by saying or doing the wrong thing. This all resulted in me pushing away many people who really loved me and wanted to help me. I trusted no one.

At that time, I had become exactly what I thought I wanted to be – a young man with a temperament who at any given time could end up in jail. Years of continuous bad behavior and undisciplined patterns, as well as hanging with the wrong crowd, caught up with me on that Friday, Nov. 30, 2007. The self-destructive acts had finally paid off.

After quitting a Division I university on a basketball scholarship and not able to keep a steady job, I joined the Marine Corps. While stationed in Miami, I received a phone call from a close friend of mine to pick up two of his friends at the Miami International Airport. Once I arrived at the airport, one of the guys mentioned that he remembered me very well, and the other had heard of me because I was once a well-known member of the Panamanian national basketball team. I knew of them as well. One was a known thug, and the other one was just a guy I would see around the city.

Well, from the airport we were on our way to South Beach to party. On our way to the beach, one of the guys received a phone call, and they asked me to stop at a nearby restaurant. I took them and patiently waited in the car thinking about all the fun we were about to have. But, I came to find out they were closing a drug deal, and 200 kilos of cocaine were inside a trunk of a nearby car where I was parked.

I found out because a few moments later, my car was surrounded by over half a dozen government vehicles and even the press. I immediately jumped out my car with my hands up and threw myself on the ground before they did. Right after they searched my car, the officers started screaming that they had found a gun and asking who was in the Marine Corps because of the uniform I had in my vehicle.

I told them it was me, and I had a permit to carry the gun. An agent walked up to me and told me that I better start talking because I was in a "world of shit." I stated that I did not know what the hell he was talking about. About 20 minutes later, they took all of us in but kept us separated. We were interrogated in separate rooms. They alternated with one agent acting like he was my friend trying to help me while the other acted just like a thug, threatening to punch mc, in which I laughed in his face.

Next were the mug shots, a strip search, and then straight to our cells. At this point, I was starting to worry. I told myself this is not looking good. I always thought guys in prison were supposed to be bad guys, but I would later find out that most of them were a bunch of snitches. Many of them had snitched on their mothers and wives to have their sentences reduced.

A few weeks had passed, and now reality had hit. I was not getting out. The relationship between me and the two other guys I was arrested with had deteriorated. They wanted me to take part in the case and claimed they would have someone deposit $40,000 into an account in Panama. Of course, I did not accept. I asked them if they thought I was stupid. I reminded them that I had nothing to do with that case, and the government did not have me on video or any recorded conversation like they had them. These so-called gangsters from Panama were collaborating with the government to have their sentence reduced by involving me in the case.

Behind my back, they were collaborating to work with the FBI to get their sentences lowered by implicating me in the case. At one point, I found myself in a scuffle that almost ended up in a fist-fight over a basketball game between me and one of the biggest guy in the detention center.

I was already giving up. I even tried to start a fight with a guard over a piece of bread. Funny right. Frustration and acceptance were settling in. On one Sunday, I went to make a collect call to my mother, who was living in New York at the time. During the call, she informed me that those two guys were making deals with the FBI and for me not to trust them. She told me to stay away from them, but as soon as I hung up with my mother, I confronted them, and of course, they denied it.

I was a little loud, and some words were exchanged. I went on to tell them that if they back-stabbed me, I would find them and make sure they paid for it if it is the last thing I do. *So not proud of that.*

The federal detention center was a one-of-a-kind experience. The sentences were so long; many inmates came back from their sentencing hearing happy to be given 10 and 15 years as if it was 10 or 15 days.

The government wanted me to plead guilty, which would keep my sentence from 13 to 18 years, but if I took them to court and lost, the sentence could be 18 to 25 years for wasting their time and money. Because I did not collaborate with the government, I was placed at the top of the list as the ring leader among the four of us. Yes, it was four of us. The other one was arrested while trying to deliver $400,000 in New York. I told my attorney to ask my mother what should I do as far as pleading guilty or taking the government to court. A few days later, my attorney told me that my mother said that she did not raise a coward.

After I had decided to fight the case, my attorney came to see me, and that's when I told him everything that I knew about the so-called witnesses to help my case. The trial went on for five days. And on a Wednesday, after all the videos and tape recordings were shown and heard in court, my name had not been heard nor was my face seen on any of the videos. When it was time to cross-examine the so-called witnesses, my attorney used that opportunity to uncover the liar by telling the jury and the judge how one of them had immigrated to the United States illegally with a fake name.

Just like that, both witnesses lost credibility, and the judge kicked them off the stand. The district attorney wanted to cross-examine me, which my attorney did not agree with. That Friday, after a decision by my mother, I decided to take the stand and answer every question the DA threw at me. Being crossed-examined by the DA was not an easy experience, but little did I know I was protected by my ancestors. Next, it was the jury's time to make a decision. It was probably the scariest moment of my life. While the jurors were making their decision, I was transported to a cell no larger than six by six feet by U.S. marshals to wait for the decision.

I had started fasting on that Monday, the day my trial began. It was now Friday, my fifth day of fasting, which made me very physically weak. I had lost about 30 pounds, and my skin had lightened up from no exposure to the sun. I remember getting on my knees and meditating, which at the time I called praying. After about a minute of meditating, I fell asleep and had a dream that told me step-by-step of what was going to happen in the next two hours. I believe now that I had tapped into the God within. That dream was a message from my ancestors telling me that everything was going to be alright.

Well, it was time for the jurors to announce their decision on the three felony counts I was charged with. When I heard the first count coming back as not guilty, I thought I was still dreaming. I was not guilty on all three counts and was ordered to be released immediately by the judge.

As I walked out the court, I panicked because I was living exactly what I had dreamed while I was awaiting the jury's decision. I tried to play it off, but everything was like *déjà* vu, and it was scary. I kept on walking, looking for my mother and my friend who had accompanied my mother throughout the entire trial. My mom then screamed out my name, which also happened in the dream. I broke down and started crying.

My mom told me not to cry and that it was over, and all I could say was that I had dreamed about all that was happening.

After my release from the federal detention center, and with the help of the Creator, my journey to live my life with a purpose had begun. I came to understand that I was not to live a self-destructive life but a life of positivity and full of purpose. It was not easy, and it still isn't, but I'm pushing toward my purpose.

I was able to get my career back, and eight months after my release, I deployed to Afghanistan. I bought my first house, became a drill instructor (which was a life-long dream), and received my bachelor's degree in Criminal Justice a month before retiring from the Marine Corps. I became a certified safety professional through a program at the University of California – San Diego and a real estate agent in California. I'm currently working on my master's in Business Administration, and I also purchased my second home.

I am now writing my first book and on my way to becoming a serial entrepreneur.

Throughout my journey, I learned I'm the director of my movie, and I can choose to not play the villain anymore. I wake up each day with a purpose in life, mentoring and inspiring anyone who might also think of destroying their life or maybe just missing that extra push to make it. I continue to push toward my goals, and I'm having fun doing it. I use my personal life experiences on a daily basis to motivate others.

I'm the director of my movie, and I will be the star of it. See you at the top.

....

BIO

Carlos D. Campbell Jr., was born in Colon City, Panama. He immigrated to the United States at the age of 14. He was a high school basketball All-American and a member of the Panamanian national basketball team. He earned an associate's degree from Southwestern College in California, and a bachelor's degree in Criminal Justice from Park University. He is currently an MBA student at the University of Phoenix, a real estate agent, and a certified safety professional. He shares his life experiences to motivate the young and the old, the rich and the poor.

10

My Grandmother's Guidance

By Kevin Thornton

My journey began New Year's Day 2006 when I wrote my yearly letter to God. In my letter, I always thank him for all blessings I had the previous year and continued blessings. That year, I asked for God to get me a job back in health insurance and to just send me where he felt would be best, and I would release all control of where I wanted to live.

On February 10, 2006, I moved to Indianapolis, where I received a job back in health insurance. God knew what he was doing by sending me to Indianapolis because the culture and lifestyle were completely different from what I was used to, so it forced me to pay more attention to my spiritual walk. Now, instead of partying on Friday nights, you could catch me at home reading a self-help or a spiritual book.

I also went back to doing the things spiritually that worked for me in the past, like journaling, creating vision boards, and meditation. During this journey, not only did I focus on my spiritual wellness but I also focused on my physical wellness. I became intrigued with holistic living and began juicing and drinking smoothies as I began to understand and believe that food heals. I also began reading a lot about nutrition and started toying with my diet. Not only did I focus on my nutrition but I started back exercising, and this was when I was introduced to indoor cycling. It was a great cardio class, and I really enjoyed it until one day the instructor did not show up, so I went and taught the class and caught the "teaching bug."

One Friday evening, my good friend and "sister" Jenita called me and told me that her grandmother's health wasn't getting any better and they didn't know how much longer she had to live. Mallie Moore, was a grandmother figure to me while I lived in Detroit, and we had a special connection. Our birthdays were a few days apart, and we were kindred spirits. It didn't help that I loved her cooking, so she lovingly called me her "eating friend."

I told Jenita I would go to Detroit next weekend to see her since we didn't know how much longer she had. The following Saturday, I went to their home, and we all sat out on the back porch talking and just enjoyed each other's company. As the visit was winding down, Grandma Moore stated how proud she was of me because she could truly see the maturity and growth in me. She went on to say that she saw me being in ministry.

Jenita and I cracked up laughing about that statement because those who knew me well knew I wasn't one for going to church, let alone being someone's minister because I loved to party and drink.

But on my way back to Indianapolis, I thought about what she said the entire drive home. When I got home, I told my cousin what was said. She also told me that she could see me as a minister; however, she added I wouldn't make any money as one because I believe holding everyone accountable for their actions, and church folks don't come to church for that.

Grandma Moore's statement made me begin searching for what my true purpose was on this planet. I meditated on it and asked God to guide me on this journey. During meditation, the Spirit spoke to me and revealed that t*o have a ministry doesn't mean you have to become a minister.*

On December 26, 2009, I received a blessing. I was relocated to Atlanta to take a better position with the company. Atlanta was always the city I wanted to live in but, God sent me there when he felt it was best for me to handle it.

Once arriving, I threw myself into my work and exercise. One Wednesday, as I was getting ready to take my boot camp class, I was listening to the Michael Baisden Show. He had Iyanla Vanzant on, and she stated that the Universe was leading her to offer a free nine-week coaching seminar for 100 men. I emailed her and became one of the 100 men. While taking the coaching seminar, I realized that what I thought my issues were was nothing compare to what the other men were going through.

The coach seminar ended up changing my life as I began to gain clarity of who I was and what I was put on this Earth to do. After completing the seminar, I realized my purpose was to become a life coach and inspire, educate, and empower others to become a greater version of themselves in mind, body, and spirit.

I research programs and enrolled in one. Part of the curriculum was to do a couple of pro-bono sessions, so I had Jenita be one of my clients. That experience prepared me for the real deal, but it also confirmed to me that this was my purpose. I loved doing it, and it did not seem like work to me. My focus began finding my niche in this field.

While getting my certificate in coaching, I was having a hard time at my corporate job. The job was stressful, and to deal with the stress, I ate and drank. My weight ballooned up to 270 pounds, and I was having back problems. The reality didn't hit me until my brother came to Atlanta for my family reunion and asked me what the problem was.

He stated that I was no longer taking my health as a priority and that I made eating wings and drinking beer my priority. It stung when he said it, but after I let it sit in my spirit, I knew what he said was right. I instantly got a trainer and began exercising and getting my diet back in order. I also learned that I was an emotional eater and had to learn how to comfort myself when under stress other than eating and drinking.

While losing weight, I got certified to become a cycling instructor. Teaching helped me in my weight-loss journey while inspiring my class. I dropped 55 pounds right in front of their eyes, which motivated them to go harder. During that time, I had eleven students get off their blood pressure medicine, and one got off his diabetic medicine due to my class and inspiration. My weight loss transformation moved one of my clients to give me the name "The Wellness Architect" as I was the designer of their health and wellness.

My mission became to inspire, educate, and motivate others to create a healthier version of themselves in mind, body, and spirit. My focus became helping others with their weight loss and getting off their medication by using food. Food and essential oils are natural ways to get healthy and heal yourself from certain ailments.

In addition, I focused educating the clients on the importance of detoxing because most people have between five and fifty pounds of feces in their body. Before anyone starts any diet or meal plan, they should detox their body first, so they can cleanse their system. Additionally, I focused on the clients getting back in balance with their primary foods: spirituality, relationships, career, and lifestyle. I taught them *when you are out of balance with one or more of the primary foods, you begin making poor eating choices. Seventy-five percent of people are emotional eaters, so they go to food for comfort when one or more of the primary foods are not in balance.*

Still asking God for guidance, I was looking for a way to touch as many people as possible other than using social media. I was blessed with the opportunity to host my own internet radio show. I never thought of myself as being a radio show host, but God knows me better than I know myself. *Walking in your purpose, the universe presents you with opportunities to do more and be more.*

In order for me to become my greatest self in my purpose, I had to step out of my comfort zone, and this was definitely out of my comfort zone. The radio show has allowed me to use the platform to teach the listeners about holistic nutrition and fitness but also changing your mindset to create the health and life you want for yourself. Also, it allowed me to use this platform to help change the narrative of what I believe society and media have created for the nation to see African American men.

I want society to know we are intelligent, hard workers, great fathers, and purposeful men. Now, once a month I do a roundtable discussion with the other male radio host of the station, and we discuss different topics. This is my way to show that men can intelligently discuss different topics other than sports and pop culture. My intention of this show is to give the listeners the tools needed to step into their power and become the greatest version of themselves and not ask permission to do so – also, to be 100 percent unapologetic for who they are and what they are trying to accomplish.

This journey is ongoing as I steadily grow to become the greatest version of myself. My only regret is that Grandma Moore is not physically here to see who I have become and the ministry I have created, but I know in my heart, she would be proud of her "eating friend."

....

BIO

Kevin Thornton has Master's degree in Organizational Psychology and certificates in life coaching and holistic health coaching. He has helped his clients lose up to 70 pounds but also get off blood pressure and diabetes medicine.

678-392-6693
Kevint211@hotmail.com
6849 Covington Hwy, Lithonia, GA 30058
www.facebook.com/holisticlifestyleconsultant

11

The Journey Ascending "Y"

By Jay Hollingshed

Ancient philosopher Pythagoras of Samos almost perfectly described my adult life through his fashioning of the letter "Y" into a pattern of human life. The vertical bottom portion of the "Y" represents the uncertainty of youth. The divide or split represents adolescence. The path to the right is difficult but leads to blessings. The easier path to the left leads to destruction.

The journey to ascending "Y" is about seeing the decisions and choosing to make them out of love, out of our souls instead of our egos…

From the outside, my adult life was good – a beautiful wife and two awesome daughters; a gorgeous home in suburban Memphis, Tennessee; fifteen years as a Memphis firefighter and EMT. I owned a successful upscale barbershop. I was active in the church choir and headed its medical ministry. I spent eight years volunteering, speaking, and training for the United Way of the Mid-South. I was even a successful runway model once. My titles spoke *success.*

In spring of 2013, God blessed my wife with a job offer in Ohio and me the opportunity to be a stay-at-home dad. By fall, we left our life in Memphis, along with all my titles. This was around the time my ego started to become more important than my family. Every decision I made after leaving selfishly benefited me. My journey had started ascending to the left side of my "Y."

I'd soon learned that when you secretly feed the smallest lie, it grows to have the biggest bite. That lie was that I could have a life separate from the family God gave me.

My ego couldn't survive Ohio, and marital problems began. So, my ego and I moved back to Memphis in July 2014. I lived off monthly installments from having sold my barbershop. It covered rent and food. I had no car note, few dishes, an air mattress, no furniture, and no plan.

Numbed by ego, I couldn't feel the pain of my family, now 600 miles away.

At the time, I didn't realize God stripped me of my titles, Memphis, and influences for a reason. I allowed my titles to nurture my ego while I neglected my soul.

My ego was simply a wrong image of myself. It started as a thought that should have been rejected, but I chose to feed it instead. As I fed the image, it grew. It outgrew my heart and became my heart when I started loving it more than my family. I depended on it for nourishment. It fed me until it consumed me. My marriage suffered because of it. Divorce papers were signed and filed, and a divorce attorney was paid in full, but no court date for the divorce proceedings was assigned yet.

While back in Memphis, partying and going to strip clubs led to my failing grad school. My repeated actions of opposing God's direction led to pain, suffering, tears, weight loss, and depression…the usual side dishes served with an entree of divorce. I looked for employment and had several interviews but no callbacks. Everything I attempted either failed or made life worse.

Tired of getting whipped by God, I surrendered completely. Right there, at my lowest point, I probably prayed the longest prayer I've ever prayed. In fact, I fell asleep praying. The scary part was when God woke me up. For the first time in my life, at age 40, God's voice was clear as 20/20 vision. It was nothing like the usual voices in my head. God said, "Go back to Ohio."

Still unsure of my purpose, I needed to be back with my family, and back in God's grace. Now, my journey started ascending the right side of the Pythagorean "Y." Before leaving Memphis, I asked God for King Solomon's wisdom to be a better father and husband. God said, "Research wisdom." The first thing I did was search "wisdom" on YouTube. A movie popped up titled, *The Secret* by Rhonda Byrne. In the movie's intro, the narrator said they had discovered the wisdom of King Solomon. I TOTALLY FREAKED OUT. I immediately fell to my knees and cried.

Since then, I've seen that movie at least 30 times, and I talk with God all day, every day. Further research revealed the depths of King Solomon's wisdom. I asked God for the humility to handle such a responsibility.

Looking back, I saw 20 years of a good lifestyle come to a screeching halt because I lost control of myself.

By Thanksgiving 2014, I was back in Ohio, and titles were no longer important. I retired my barber's license in Tennessee. I've had no desire to practice emergency medicine or firefighting. My former connections and influences are beyond my reach in Memphis.

I was positioned to rely solely on God.

I took that time and studied other wise men, spiritual gurus, swamis, and positive world influencers. Mahatma Gandhi, Jesus of Nazareth, Siddhārtha Gautama (Buddha), Krishna, Muhammad, and the Dalai Lama are just a few. I read books that inspired these wise men and the books they inspired or wrote – the Bible, Bhagavad-Gita, Guru Granth Sahib, Kabbalah, Kyogyoshinsho, Quran, and the Torah. While studying these culturally-biased books of moral law, I learned much of the world's six major religions: Buddhism, Christianity, Hinduism, Islam, Judaism, and Sikhism. I identified with their wisdom and their teachings of peace, righteousness, love, and respect for a deity. They have a common denominator, but they differ in culture, doctrine, and dogma. I adopted the common denominator as my way of life and put aside argumentative doctrines, dogma and opinion. Becoming one with God and not religion has become my spiritual foundation.

From there, I studied the 12 Immutable Universal Laws. I gained a lot of information of their relationship to man. During my studies, God kept my eyes upward and away from spiritual mirrors until I was ready to find God instead of ego when looking in them. I was growing spiritually, but I still wasn't yet the husband and father God wanted me to be.

By now, I had a ton of information to convert into knowledge. I had to be reprogrammed. I went through a process of *Learning How to Learn,* as Dr. Clifford Black would say.

As spiritual beings in physical bodies, we're meant to live and learn from the inside out.

Everything I'd learned up until then was from the outside in. I had 40 years of backward learning to undo. For example, I spent time looking and hearing when I should have been seeing and listening. My five senses were influenced by other people's touch, smell, hearing, sight, and taste. I rarely consulted my own, God-led intuitive discretion for what naturally agrees with my spirit. In short, I was educated by an external atmosphere that didn't internally know me. Soon, I learned to trust my instincts and act on what appeals to my highest sense of truth and morality.

I finally found God when looking in the mirror, and my journey continued ascending Pythagorean's "Y." My purpose of teaching the principles of my experience was slowly unveiling itself. I began the mental process of learning to teach others how to connect with the "Genius/Genie" within themselves as did the wise leaders I'd been studying.

I reconnected with the teachings of my past master and good friend, Bobby C. Pearson Sr. of Memphis. Twenty years ago, Pearson taught me that I could use my mind to be a millionaire in five years if I so desired. Pearson's teachings were congruent with my current teacher, mentor, and philosopher Dr. Clifford Black, also of Memphis.

Understanding the mental process of learning, Dr. Black started me on a curriculum of mental sciences that included epistemology, etiology, etymology, and ontology, among other subjects. His teachings of philosophy and psychology navigated me through the processes of the human mind and the understandings of consciousness. This stabilized my ***J****ourney* ***A****scending* "**Y**." The more I studied, my hunger for understanding grew. My goals evolved as I evolved. My senses heightened as my vision expanded. God was revealing my purpose as I became one with my studies. Not sure if such a title exists, but I was starting to feel like a "mental optometrist."

God made me a stay-at-home dad allowing me time to devote six hours a day, six days a week for three years toward my purpose. Philosophers and psychologists like Socrates, Plato, Aristotle, Friedrich Nietzsche, Ivan Pavlov, and Abraham Maslow used to bore me. Now, I read and reread them discovering something new about myself each time. I started converting my mass of information into knowledge and a great deal of that knowledge into wisdom. Repetitive applications of wisdom continue to feed my hunger and give me understanding.

My journey has resulted in some of the most beautiful decisions I've ever made as a man, father, husband, brother, son, and leader. Now, I purposely look for and create opportunities for others. There was a time when I'd come across $500 and head straight to the mall and go crazy spending it to appease my ego and those who influenced my five senses. (I recently came across $500, and I still went crazy.)

To be specific, I used Jim Rohn's 70-10-10-10 percentage rule for financial success, spending my entire seventy percent on books! That was my reality check. I'm certainly not that dude I used to be.

When driving, I rarely listen to music. It's either audiobooks or affirmations. Not having funds to travel to various psychology and personal development seminars doesn't stop me. I attend three to four online seminars per week on YouTube as I continue to feed my growing hunger for understanding.

I started my business and career approximately 24 months ago. I spent 18 months of that time maximizing free social media outlets to aggressively brand myself and maintain relevance.

My purpose now is to teach the science of personal development in such a manner that it empowers businesses and people. My business vision is to be the Mental Performance Coach of choice for celebrities, A-Listers, business moguls, entertainers, and athletes. My personal vision is to be an impactful philanthropist. I possess an ounce of faith, a ton of ambition, and the audacity to be unstoppable! When I'm done moving mountains, my introduction will be:

"Hi! I'm Jay Hollingshed, billionaire philanthropist. I travel the world teaching the science and application of mental performance. By doing so, I help manifest blessings for all mankind, and I do so with love. Here's my card. How can I be a blessing to you today?"

This **J***ourney* **A***scending* **"Y"** can teach you what it taught me, that enlightenment is a shift in self-identification – an awareness of what and who we are which is love.

Jay Hollingshed isn't beautiful. God empowering others through Jay Hollingshed is beautiful. Thank you, Saba Tekle and 7-Publishing, for selecting me and giving me the opportunity to be a blessing. I'm honored to be one of your *20 Beautiful Men.*

BIO

James (Jay) Hollingshed is the owner of *jayHOLLiNGSHED®, LLC,* where he coaches and teaches mental performance, is a Certified Executive Coach, Life Coach, and Speaker. He has a bachelor's degree in Organizational Development, a master's degree in Health Care Administration, and has been accepted to start courses for his Doctor of Education in Sport and Performance Psychlogy. He volunteers weekly at the Community Kitchen of Columbus and is a volunteer mentor & board member for the nonprofit organization All THAT – Teens Hopeful About Tomorrow.

12

Standing Man

By Joe Ballard

I learned the Russian word *Правозащитник* from watching Tom Hanks' classic *Bridge of Spies*. It was used in the movie aesthetically. It translates to "standing man" – someone who will stand up and remain battle-ready against insurmountable difficulties without caving in, whether in defending justice, truth, a loved one, a cause, or confronting a physical dilemma or plight.

In the movie, Tom Hanks was the "standing man." I believe *Bridge of Spies* resonates with the warrior within each of us who keeps fighting against all odds until we win. The movie also highlights the question of whether an individual has the courage, strength, and fortitude to remain a standing man (or woman) while facing a precarious situation. That is, can one remain resolute in the midst of substantial, unpleasant conditions, especially a serious, sad, or dilemma that threatens your very life?

I have said over the years that circumstances don't make the man as much as they reveal him to himself. Often, I've reminded myself that there is so much more happening in me, than there is ever happening to me. Something good is cooking inside the pot while the fire burns hot.

It was this epic tidbit of wisdom that brought me strength after being kicked in the groin by a horse while working on a farm in rural North Lawrence, Ohio. Being raised in the inner city of Chicago, Illinois, the only conversation I'd ever had about horses was when I'd ask my mother, Lucile. "Where are you going so early?"

Dawning a bright smile, she replied, "To see a man about a horse." I assumed that had to be a mama's sense of humor.

After a few months of being kicked, I noticed an unfamiliar knot had sprung up on my buttocks. It took on the form of a strange, painful hair bump the size of a pinhead, unlike a pimple or hives. After about a year, I noticed a recurrent boil-like lump that would come every other month and culminate in pus-like discharges that multiplied by 2's and 3's. By the fifth year, I was unable to remain seated for any period of time due to excruciating pain.

Being married at the time, I'd wake up in a pool of blood and would intentionally stay in bed until my wife got up so I could secretly change the sheets. I was riddled with shame. I hid this condition for years from everyone including my best friend – Lucile – my mother who told me jokes about horses. I told no one. I suffered in silence despite the unbearable agony. Men are notorious for their silent sufferings.

It was my secret to keep but god's secret to reward!

Matthew 6:6 tells us, "When you pray, go into your most private room, close the door, and pray to the Father who is in secret, and your Father who sees (what is done) in secret will reward you openly."

Within six years, that tiny hair bump grew and multiplied into 22 pus-like discharges, unable to heal, open wounds. While my faith grew, I was blessed to travel to 38 nations and six continents and train over 70,000 leaders – igniting passion and healing wounded hearts by the grace of God. The open reward of a standing man!

Have you ever asked a question when you already knew the answer?

After six years of pain, I consulted three doctors from three states. Each of whom agreed to somehow remedy my pain. But upon viewing my condition, they vehemently said, "Joe, this is not what I thought it was. There is nothing anyone can do. It's too far gone.

You have about six months to live." I soon discovered that I had consulted with the wrong three doctors. Now don't get it twisted. While I didn't know the outcome, I thought, "If my end is near, I'm going out with a bang while blazing a trail. I'm a standing man, a game-changer.

"MIRROR, MIRROR ON THE WALL, I WILL ALWAYS STAND UP AFTER I FALL. AND WHETHER I RUN, WALK, OR HAVE TO CRAWL... I HAVE SET MY GOALS, AND I WILL ACHIEVE THEM ALL." – UNKNOWN

Despite the doctors' reports, I learned relentlessness is a game-changer. Despite my chronic disease, I became relentless in pursuit of my dreams. I didn't tell myself, "You're going to die in six months." What I saw in my heart was what I said until what I said was what I saw in my life! I absolutely refused to see a casket in the grave; instead, I saw myself as an acorn becoming an oak tree. No matter what came my way, I remained true to the only thing we all have, and that's ourselves.

When you are true to yourself, great things can happen. In fact, with every bad thing we face, God can redeem it and made it good. The enemy of your soul can't win for losing. God has a way of promoting us through adversity, attacks, and pain.

I had become an international speaker and foreign ambassador (despite the unimaginable agony and pain I suffered) in an effort to go big or go home.

I accepted the impossible task of absolute servanthood to my goals and dreams to infuse greatness, ignite passion, and leave a legacy, and it changed my entire life!

You see, to become a standing man, it starts with a burning desire in your heart to become one with your dreams. Next, decide to use your life story as a platform for good. Finally, don't lose yourself when hell hits hard; you can be a better you than pretending to be somebody else. The most important thing is to be true to yourself.

Being true to yourself allows people to begin to see the path of your pain at work, and the grass-roots everyday activity of the journey you took on the road to greatness. Though the journey that makes us all awesome is interestingly unique, our pain is the same; our human experience is the same. Pain is the toughest thing to deal with, but at the same time, it can be the best thing to fuel your destiny and dreams.

Imagine being unable to remain seated due to pain during five- to 15-hour international flights. Imagine having a constant cycle of blood flow three weeks every other month for five years. Imagine a recurrent open wound that grew by 2's and 3's – boil-like lumps that culminated into a bloody mass. Now, imagine a relentless determination to fulfill your dreams until they come alive within you. This was my secret sauce to success – my path to greatness. My pain plagued me until my dreams began to live through me.

Listen, something incredible shifts within when you are confronted with your own immortality (whether sickness, death, poverty or divorce). For some, it's utter hopelessness, but for others, it's absolute hope. The beauty is you get to choose. When you seize hope, life takes on eternal significance. Like a man standing above the trees, you see the forest clearly for the very first time. You sacrifice the trivialities of pride, ego, doubts, and self-imposed fears for the tangible essence of life, liberty, and legacy. Standing man (woman), boy (girl) let radical hope open to you a new chapter of limitless possibilities.

So, how do you begin to enjoy limitless possibilities? Proverbs 18:21 tells us, "The tongue has the power of life and death, and those who love it will eat its fruit." I began to speak life to the disease in me. "Joseph, you will outlive this evil disease... It's not stronger than you – You are stronger than it. RELENTLESS – YOU WILL LIVE

TO THE END OF NEXT YEAR." Believe me, it's the story you tell yourself that determines what manifests in your life.

According to your mustard seed faith, no mountain can stand in your way. You see, faith appeals to heaven's court – a higher realm of reality – and knows that heaven has rendered a verdict of good despite seeming difficulties. By faith, everything you need is inside of you; it's not the external that defines you – it's your internal core that produces great results.

IN LIFE, IT'S NOT THAT YOU ARE DEALT A BAD HAND – IT'S YOUR ABILITY TO PLAY A BAD HAND WELL – UNKNOWN

So play the hand life deals to you because no challenge can match the heart, fight, and spirit of a made-up mind. Once a mind is pregnant with a new idea, it never aborts or fails to deliver. At the end of the eight-year fight, not even the Hidradenitis suppurativa (a chronic malignant tumor) could continue to stand against a standing man's faith. It's been 17 blissful years since my plight with that malignant tumor clinging to my body. There isn't a day that goes by in which I am not eternally grateful for being one who stood in the midst of such a struggle. To the millions who continue to suffer in silence, believe me, there is a rainbow at the end of the journey.

Final thoughts: What would you do if you knew you couldn't fail? Again, how you see yourself determines your outcome. Decide that you are relentless, brilliant, and beautiful. It's true; who you are is not the result of what others say to you or what happens to you on your road to greatness. Who you are is the result of what you continually say to yourself – I AM A STANDING MAN!

Beautifully Standing Man,
Joe Ballard.

....

BIO

Joe Ballard, an international speaker, author, licensed dream coach, and leadership trainer, is the CEO and president of Harvest International Network, LLC – an all-encompassing network of leadership training with headquarters in Chicago, Illinois. He is also the founder of Urdream Academy, a coaching institute designed to elevate the masses to achieve massive success. Joe holds a B.S. in Accounting and Business Administration and an M.A. in Theology and Leadership Concepts.

Having served as a senior pastor for over 25 years while training nearly 70,000 leaders worldwide, Joe has traveled extensively throughout the United States, Canada, Europe, Russia, Africa, South America, and Israel. His purpose is to ignite the gift of passion in people spiritually, socially, and physically – unleashing them to fulfill their ultimate destiny. A man whose message has been heard around the world, Joe is committed to lifting the veil of limitation and opening the portal to the God-given potential in every person.

13

Where There's a Will There's a Way

By William Harrison

How the heck did I end up in this book? I don't know about the other 19 men, but I don't think there's anything beautiful about my story... that's what I thought until I looked back on my life. I pray that the words you are about to read help you overcome your own challenges and help you reach your greatest potential.

Growing up, I never felt like I fit in with the other kids in my neighborhood or at school. Being an introvert and shy made it tough for me to open up. Often, I would be in deep thought analyzing the world around me. Unfortunately, I didn't understand this nor did the kids at school. Thus, I endured lots of ridicule for being different. I guess today you might consider it bullying. Even at an early age it didn't take me long to realize the world could be a cruel place. We are punished for being unique.

Looking back, the one person I really connected with was my grandfather. Despite a 60-year age gap, he and I developed a deep bond. He never said much, but I really looked up to him. To this day I see his influence over me, even down to the way I dress. Grandpa Bup, that was his nickname, had to be the most influential person in my life. As long as I can remember he would get up at the crack of dawn to go outside and work in the yard just before he read the local news with his cup of coffee. I never remember him complaining. He worked tirelessly up until the time of his death. Bup was the father figure that I needed. Without saying much, he provided me a reference point for manhood. I dare think of where I would be had he not been in my life. Somedays I wish he could see the man I became. Shortly before I started high school my grandfather passed away. With no male guidance to lead me through my teenage years, life got real.

Donald Glover from the FX series "Atlanta" sums up my high school years best, "I felt like high school was like a big whirlpool of me trying to figure out what was OK for me to do." High school is challenging for everyone, particularly when you are trying to find your own identity. *For African-American boys, I think it's even tougher to figure out who we are. Many of us don't have fathers in our homes and we are left with what we see on TV and around our neighborhood to define who we are.*

When I was in high school in the 80s, crack cocaine took over my community. Even the young drug dealers in my neighborhood had expensive cars, and some even purchased homes for their families. As tempting as it seemed, I couldn't resort to selling drugs. For one, my momma would have killed me and jail wasn't the place to be. Above everything else, I felt deep inside that there was more to life than fancy cars and quick cash. While some of my friends were establishing themselves in the drug game, I started requesting college brochures. Even though my grades weren't the best, I knew that college was the right choice for me. Before I knew it, my senior year had arrived and I was one step closer to graduation. At the astonishment of some, I was accepted into my school of choice. Not knowing what to expect, I was off to college leaving behind the world I'd come to know so well in exchange for a new life full of its own challenges. An opportunity to spread my wings and fly had finally come.

College was my first taste of true freedom and I wasn't ready for it at all. It wasn't because of the workload or how challenging the work was. I simply didn't have the study habits or discipline needed to be successful. Unlike high school, I couldn't just *wing it.* College required studying and taking notes. Despite my dismal performance in the classroom, I connected with a group of guys who I still call friends. I guess I connected with them because we were all minority students in a predominantly white school. This was a culture shock for me because my high school was close to 98 percent African-American. I was never intimidated, but it was an eye opener. One of the biggest regrets I have is that early in my college career I didn't apply myself enough. After a few mediocre semesters, I transferred to a junior college back home. I didn't stay home long as I improved my grades and went off to another four-year university. It was in my junior year that I realized my life needed a change as I began to worry about my increasing student loan debt. Just like I've done all my life, I decided to take a chance on me.

To this day, I don't know why I contacted a military recruiter. He suggested I give the military a try. The few people I confided in suggested I should not join the military. In fact, some didn't think I was tough enough to handle it. I'm so glad I didn't listen to them. Joining the military was the best thing I could have done. The military added the one ingredient I was missing in my life, and that was discipline.

The moment you join the military, you learn how to multi-task quickly. Once you learn how to shower, get dressed, and make a bed up all in 5 minutes, you soon realize you can do almost anything. I owe all my success to my time served in the military. There was one quote I memorized while in the military. It helped me get through many of the challenging times I faced. It went something like this. "Not every day is good. But there is something good in everyday".

After serving my country, I made my way into Corporate America. I thought the military was tough, but Corporate America is a beast of its own. You may wonder, how so? Well, in the military, everything is either black or white. You know who's in charge, and you understand all the rules that govern what you do. That's not the case at most companies. Of course, people have titles, but you have no idea (at least initially) who has the power.

My first day out of uniform and into a crisp three button suit, I felt like a fish out of water. Like many veterans who turn in their boots for loafers, we experience a culture shock once we leave the service for any other line of work. I was no different. I even doubted myself. It was like I was starting life all over again. After about a year into corporate life, I realized all the training I received in the military had prepared me for my new challenge.

Simply put, I had to stick my chest out and face my fears. Not long after that, I began to feel comfortable in my own skin. Eventually, I went on to have a great career in several well-known companies in various roles. With all that said, I still felt like something was missing.

A new challenge awaited me, but I didn't know what it was, yet. If you have made it this far in my story, I think you know where this is going. I decided to make another life detour. This time, it was in the form of entrepreneurship.

I thought I had experienced it all until the day I decided to start my own management consulting business. Nothing can prepare you for entrepreneurship. It's almost like having a baby. You can read all the books about it, but until you go through it, you have no idea what it's like. That's how I felt when I gave up my corporate gig. At that point of my life, I wanted more control over what I did. No longer would I have someone telling me what assignments or projects to take on. Instinctively, I knew that I was more than able to go out and make it on my own.

I had no idea how hard it is making it on your own. It didn't take long for me to realize entrepreneurship requires everything you have. There are no days off, and it's on you if things don't get done. Some days, I feel like I'm on an emotional rollercoaster going from the highest of highs to the lowest of lows within the same hour, but I wouldn't trade it for anything in the world. I enjoy the challenge of finding new clients and building my company. I haven't made it big quite yet, but considering my track record, I think it's only a matter of time. Just like I overcame bullying, a tough neighborhood, and my own insecurities, I plan on adding entrepreneurship to the list.

So, there you have it, my beautiful story of finding my identity, overcoming failure, and most importantly laying it all on the line to chase my dreams. We may never get the chance to meet, but hopefully something I said resonated with you. Don't let your beginning determine your end. You'd be amazed at what you could accomplish if you simply take that one step of faith. I'm living proof of that. Every day I force myself to take on a new challenge. You should do the same. It only takes a determined will. In the words of John Quincy Adams, "Patience and perseverance have a magical effect before which difficulties and obstacles vanish." Best of luck, my friend.

Thank you for reading my chapter. I would love to keep the discussion going. If you would like to know more about me or hear more of my unique perspective please visit thereallifewill.com or send an email to will@thereallifewill.com. Make sure to follow me on Twitter @9thPrez. I'm also available for consulting projects, speaking engagements and any contributing editor or guest blog requests.

....

BIO

As a self-proclaimed introvert, Will always found solace in his own thoughts growing up. He found it hard to find his identity in a tough neighborhood where there were many distractions. Through hard work, self-determination, and God's grace, Will overcame a challenging start and found his purpose. After a successful military and corporate career, Will now focuses all his efforts on entrepreneurial endeavors, public speaking and his first love, writing.

14

Faith Without Works

By Dr. Ladre Weathersby

In March 1990, we went to the beautiful Our Lady of the Snows spiritual retreat center for a time of great spiritual focus and renewal. We had gone to fellowship with other believers in a setting of snow-capped hills, a lake, and utopian serenity – the chance to meet God and refocus on what matters produced peace. However, that peace and bliss quickly turned to devastation and violation. Why? That weekend gave thieves time to clean us out at home. EVERYTHING of any value was gone…except the kitchen sink. They even swiped my $2 bill hidden in my wallet. My little 9-year-old heart was crushed, especially as I proudly boasted we were going away for vacation.

The worst part of it all was my parents' response. *Trust God.* Everything was left up to Him. That was one of three hugely impressionable events that created my philosophy. You see, I completely believed in God doing miracles, and even His part, but I later admitted that all I saw was *Faith (believing God) without works (doing my part) is dead.* So at that time, watching my parents sit back and do nothing left me confused.

The second childhood event occurred later that same summer of 1990. We struggled so hard financially that my older brother and I learned how to take 'quarter baths' from pots of hot water heated on the electric hot plate. It only took about ten minutes, so we ironed our clothes or ate breakfast while we waited. We also learned something about 'put-together meals.' You'd put together everything edible and eat it like it was a coordinated and planned meal (Lol). However, this day was very different…

This time we came home to a dark house AND no gas. Imagine not being able to see or cook. You couldn't read a book after dark as the house of candles made it too cumbersome to move around. Thankfully, it was the summer, so we didn't have to worry about heat. Nevertheless, we were then shipped over to Grandpa's house for the weekend and always *recovered* but never got ahead. How could we when, a couple of years later, my mom's two part-time jobs showed just $1,277 in monthly income on my lunch form? I still wonder to this day how we survived. That financial struggle repeated itself throughout my childhood and was prevalent in my entire family; it gave me a strong poverty mindset.

That was my upbringing. My loving, caring family WANTED a better life, but we were imprisoned by poverty and spiritual imbalance that I didn't truly recognize until I grew older. We spent more time in church than we spent learning about money, health, and the other parts of life that were so key. But I learned that overly relying on God is different from needing a miracle.

In March 2002, while a senior at Morehouse College, that point was proved.

This young, strapping, healthy 21-year-old college student became deathly ill in a matter of days. Days of fever, chills, and diarrhea eventually led me to the emergency room. After I had been sent home, things worsened. Unable to stand for long with blood-colored urine and yellow eyes and skin, I went back to the emergency room and was admitted.

My irreplaceable mother magically appeared by my side because I was admitted to the hospital and it didn't look good. Bad health numbers continued to rise, and nurses apologized as I needed a liver and a kidney transplant. The search began immediately for a donor, and psychiatric evaluations were ordered. However, with nothing we could humanly do, hundreds of people all across the country bombarded heaven. First, there was no change, and that lasted for almost a week. Then, HEAVEN RESPONDED! The Emory University Hospital doctors were baffled. Something, maybe the medicine, *finally* started working. Health numbers began to decline, and answers to "Why?" were no longer needed. However, no cause could be found. I even blamed my last meal I cooked of smothered meatballs, carrots, and mashed potatoes, which I didn't eat again for almost a year (Yes, Beautiful Men can cook too, lol). After eleven days in the intensive care unit, I made a total recovery…with a medical bill just shy of $100K! Thank God for health insurance. Yet, after that miracle, I was still confused.

After college, I began my financial journey in October 2004, but even with a good job as a teacher, everything did not fall in line. I saw people making better money as did I, but I still lacked basic financial literacy. Growing up, my parents and I never had a sit-down conversation about money, credit, relationships, etc. Left to my own devices, I quickly repeated my parents' patterns.

Instead of cooking, I'd eat or order out, which costs so much more for the convenience. I would finally go shopping, but not financially plan the entire spending experience. I didn't create an emergency fund for the times when 'life happened,' and often my bad decisions caused problems. That behavior, compounded with others, forced me to the pawn shop with my newish laptop and household appliances. I was completely devastated by the pennies on the dollar I was offered for my valuables.

Did they not recognize the hard work, agony, sweat, and tears to acquire those things? I learned the hard way what really makes something an asset. Just because I saw value in something did not make it an asset that could be traded for cash in the marketplace (gym shoes, car rims, hair weave, and cheap furniture).

Unfortunately, in the fall of 2014, after rebuilding my credit, buying a home, co-signing for other people to get stuff and so many other things, I was at that place AGAIN. Although, this time it wasn't because of the then-current relationship. For the second time, I decided to no longer teach high school English and build my own business, but I still lacked the consistent, disciplined work ethic to succeed. Sometimes, I'd play games too long or easily get distracted and not keep the main thing as the main thing. I was overwhelmed and not as prepared as I thought. It was so much easier to do that when it was a job. Doing it for myself, on the other hand, was completely different and very scary.

I saw time and time again where poverty mindedness showed up. It produced two bankruptcies (for different reasons), multiple closed bank accounts, experiences running from the repo man, dodging collection calls from seemingly everybody for bills, a time on food stamps as a grown man, huge chunks of income thrown away to bank fees, and learning how to get an apartment with bad credit. I look back at my financial records today and see the lack of a budget, just hoping and praying that everything would work out. Clearly, that was NOT working based on the results I had.

So how is my life completely different now and still getting better?

First, I learned to proactively take responsibility for EVERYTHING. My parents were reactive to everything and laid it on God to fix. However, personal growth taught me that I could change things for the better with my own intentional actions. I willingly took responsibility for my prior actions and their current results.

In March 2015, I filed for Chapter 7 bankruptcy again but vowed never to do that again. I had to learn to be okay with where I am, but not stay there. I wanted to earn higher wages, but the market doesn't place the higher value on the skills I had as a teacher. So, I decided to really work on being self-employed. It was a daily struggle against the old, limiting poverty mindset, but I no longer placed the blame for my bad decisions on others.

Finally, I took serious time for mentors and coaches – people farther along than I, who had the lifestyle I desired. I wholeheartedly believe that *being stuck* simply means we haven't found or applied the solution. In video games, before you get to level 3, you MUST complete level 2. It has the access point, but sometimes it's hidden or disguised in a way that your eye has to be trained to see. That's where mentors and coaches come in. My first mentor type was my AP English teacher, Mrs. Bettye Jean Miller. She was a TASKMASTER! I remember her tearing up someone's work in front of the ENTIRE class. She refused to accept less than our best. She knew many of us came from disadvantaged homes and circumstances, but she cared less about those factors like drive-by shootings, neighborhood drug dealing and gangs, and more.

My first CHOSEN mentor happened much later.

Why choose a mentor? They help refine the WAY we see what we see. The difference between the wealthy and ultra successful is often HOW they perceive the same things everyone else sees. They see opportunities where the masses see problems. They see untapped potential where others see the limitation. They see long-term blessings and benefits, while some only see short-term pain. One of my mentors always said, "Some things you just don't know." It's true, but I took forever to accept it and forgive myself for some of the prior mistakes I made. They shaped my vision, prepared a new perspective, and pushed my passion.

My mentors helped me see more clearly. As I said earlier, my parents relied totally on God without playing a part I could see for myself. My mentors taught me that God is there to help add his *super* to my *natural.* It was my job to learn and do all that I could with better skills and effort. God would then add to my preparation for success.

My mentors also helped me discover my purpose and passion in life. How did I mess up so much? I often didn't know any better. Our education system molds us to be wrong for what we don't know, but the real problem is what we REFUSE to learn and then apply. I simply played the hand I was dealt, to the best of my ability. I hadn't yet learned that, in many ways, I could pick some of the cards I had based on my personal choices. I became an avid reader of things that would add value to my life today and help me not just get over my past but guide me toward my true purpose, not society's vision.

My mentors (in person and via books, CDs, and seminars) showed me that I could have it ALL! I didn't have to settle for a sliver of the pie. I could have the finances to live as I please, the health to do as I please, and the quality relationships with myself and others who support me going forward without holding me back. I could have the social life to experience the best life has to offer, the cultural experiences of new and different things, the spiritual connection to the Divine Father, a career that impacts people while producing income, and a progressive intellectual and emotional intelligence that will help me be a better person. I keep pursuing the better life and see it happening before my eyes (thanks to my journal). I am proud of my progress, but there is so much more ahead for me. If you start and continue on your journey, the same will be said by you too. Be encouraged, be expanded, and be implanted in the experience. Life is worth the living!

....

BIO

Dr. Ladre Weathersby is a business owner, coach, speaker and trainer. With advanced degrees from Mercer and Capella Universities, he encourages, enlightens and "edutrains" thousands as a certified life coach. His sessions challenge participants to dig deep and be transparent, while giving tools to help themselves, instead of developing a dependence on others. Available for booking, he resides in Atlanta, Georgia.

FB @LadreWeathersby & Better Life Institute
Twitter @bettalifecoach
Youtube @betterlifeinstitute
www.betterlifeinstitute.info
ladreweathersby@gmail.com

15

The Catalyst - Unconditional Love

By Brian Carter

I can remember sitting in my room upstairs in the attic, sulking, after I first heard my parents tell me they were getting divorced. Even at the age of ten, I already knew it was coming. Maybe it was my fault. Was I too emotional, hyper, or… I just didn't know.

The car ride down to Virginia with my father and sister became one of my first turning points in life. It was quiet most of the time. I wanted to ask questions but didn't know what to ask. By that time, I had lived in over fifteen different places – leaving friends behind was typical, but now I was saying goodbye to my mother. I conceded a notion that leaving places and people was a normal part of life.

I didn't settle into the new changes quickly, but eventually, I started to open up. My father remarried, and with the help of my stepmother Karyn and a few friends in high school (including my dear friend Ryan who sadly passed away a few years later), Virginia became home.

After undergrad studies, I found myself without a sense of identity. I was spending more money than I had and partying too often. I was mentally checked out with the pressure of jumping into a career without knowing who I was. The relationship I invested in was over, and to top it all off, my family was once again at risk with my father and stepmother getting divorced.

I watched families fall apart my entire life, and frankly, I didn't want to see it again. At that point, I felt that I had two options: stay and deal with the s**t show or get as far away as possible. So I packed my car, subleased my room in Virginia, and moved to Florida. Florida had the sunshine, beaches, and a lengthy 1,000 miles from the drama of my life in Virginia.

The first few months, I was at a low fighting depression, disappointment, and the pent-up rage. I had a chip on my shoulder that I was tired of. Instead of going back to partying and ignoring the facts of my life, I began to write. It started with simple words in notes and on scraps of paper and eventually led into what I was doing in Florida, the people I'd met, and how this transition had been.

Eventually, I began to follow Elite Daily, an online publisher for Millennials to share their experiences in life, dating, and so on. I would reflect on other thoughts and continue to write for myself. *Oh, and by the way, I tested the dating tips for picking up women, and they worked at least ten percent of the time.*

I kept expanding my reading, and eventually, the book "The Alchemist" by Paulo Coelho fell into my hands. After reading about the main character's journey, I knew I was in search for my personal legend (the unique path that leads to an individual's destiny). Passionate about my next steps, I got ahold of Elite Daily and asked to write for them. They accepted my proposal and allowed me to publish articles on their website. While my first article was about why a millennial man should date an older woman (yes, this was a real experience, and I knew it would catch the attention of the Elite Daily publishers), I later transformed my writings to inspire myself, along with others.

I enjoyed writing for a large publisher; however, in late February, I felt it was time to branch off to create a blog for myself. I reached out to my friend Nicole who I had met in a bar playing wingman. Inspired to start a blog, I pitched an idea to her about how we could write about the different perspectives of men and women on the topic that no one talks about – healthy relationships. She quickly agreed.

The vision was to share our experiences in hopes to learn more about the opposite sex and what it meant to be in a healthy relationship. As we grew together, our brand evolved from "He Said or She Said" to "The Unguarded Heart." We created a place for ourselves to live a vulnerable and unguarded life. And that we did. My friendship and partnership with Nicole became the healthiest relationship I had with a woman. It allowed me to understand myself while learning to communicate with the opposite sex in a platonic relationship (shocker). The Unguarded Heart opened my career, relationships, and life to amazing things.

During the mix of everything, Nicole introduced me to a dear friend of hers named Mo. I can always remember the exact feeling and memory of sitting down with Mo for lunch that first time. I was drawn to her warm energy, and I knew there was something about her that I wanted in my life. Mo, Nicole, and I continued to grow our companionship by involving each other in our online businesses. We would often meet at Mo's house and have our brainstorming sessions – discussing our next big thing, personal and professional growth, or simply enjoying each other's company.

Mo was a guardian angel – a mentor and friend I had not expected. My relationship with Mo grew over the span of many months while I was bouncing back and forth between jobs. Unhappy and still looking to find a career path that suited me, I decided to give Mo a call one day. After the panic had poured out, Mo paused and asked if I was ready to jump. Well, that scared me to the core. I was already broke and barely holding onto things. I responded, "There's no way I could do that." She told me that I must leap, have faith and that I will figure it out...especially if I really wanted it. It scared the crap out of me to leave the scraps I was getting by on, but eventually, I did.

A few weeks later, I left my sales job to split my time working for Mo and picking up shifts at Starbucks. Since Mo was a career coach and I wanted to get further into technology, the plan was for me to help her with the digital fronts of her business – creating pamphlets, marketing on social media, and tweaks to her website. It was a punch to my ego working as a barista and making less money than I did when I was 16, but I felt this sense of freedom that couldn't be replaced.

I continued to freelance, and eventually, I started my own tech company with someone I had met at a personal development course. Many people ask how I started my first company. They ask what the steps were, how did I prepare for it, and so on. I always respond the same: "You just jump."

Perhaps one of my favorite parts of my journey was what came next. While working with Mo and starting my independent freelancing career, I was introduced to Jennifer. Jennifer was a national author and business owner. After our initial conversations, she offered me work, and eventually, we became strategic partners. We worked together for quite some time, having done wonderful business together. It was in this relationship and partnership that my journey had made its first full circle.

Going back to that personal development course I mentioned earlier: During one of the courses, an instructor spoke about how as parents if we are going through some difficulties in a relationship with our partner, we still show our kids unconditional love and support. Here's the kicker…

After my parents first divorced, I decided not to talk to my mother for over six years. I had been cutting people out my entire life. It was just easier that way. For those many years, she sent me letters and called and left voicemails, which I never returned. I'm not sure what it was, but during my junior year of college, I decided to respond to her. Perhaps it was curiosity or another shift in my life, regardless, I am glad I did. Over the years, we developed a new relationship that I am infinitely grateful for. And here is the best part – this experience did more than re-create our relationship.

A couple of years after working with Jennifer, we had a long conversation. At first, we spoke about business and expansion (which was always very exciting), but right before we hung up, the conversation shifted as she said, "Brian, I want to thank you." At first, I figured she was pleased with our work together. That was until she began to talk about a small conversation we had over a year before. At the time, she and her husband were going through a divorce, and her children did not want to have a relationship with her. She was in a rut and asked for my advice. Between my experience with my mother and hearing it again at that course, I told her to love them unconditionally and to not make it about her – they needed to know she was there to support them through the divorce. She went on to tell me that she took my advice and that she and her kids were talking again. I was in awe – speechless.

This is what unconditional love does.

It changed the relationship between my mother and me, and that same love from one of my deepest struggles became the catalyst in healing someone else's relationship with their children. Healing our wounds has an impact on the world around us. I believed for a long time that my purpose was to impact millions of lives. These lessons have taught me that life isn't about how many lives we impact; it's about how deeply we impact those lives.

This is the purpose of our journey on Earth, to love and be loved – to heal and to be healed.

Many years later as I write these words, I am in a profession I love – creating really cool things – just like I did as a kid. In August 2016, I stepped away from The Unguarded Heart as it was time for my next journey. To this day, Nicole and I are best friends still sharing our worlds with each other.

Thank you, to all of my parents, siblings, friends, and coworkers for the unconditional love over the years. In the words of a song that says it so well, "In these bodies, we will live; in these bodies, we will die, and where you invest your love, you invest your life."

....

BIO

I've always sought to create, explore and understand why things are the way they are and how to expand them into something else. I was often told that between my ADHD and my extremely low reading and writing levels, I wouldn't make it in school and to strive for mediocrity. Instead of listening to others, I've led with my heart through my journey. Now I express openly, endeavor in many business ventures...and yeah, I graduated from my master's program as the Salutatorian.

Feel free to reach out, follow, and connect with me:

Social: IG//FB: @itsbcarter //
https://www.linkedin.com/in/itsbcarter
bacarter9@yahoo.com
http://itsbcarter.com/

16

What Defines A Man?
The Fight to Find Identity

By Hayward Renard Miller Jr.

Have you ever had the feeling of chasing something your entire life, and with every good thing that comes, it brings you closer, but you still feel like it's hard for you to obtain it?

For most of us, pursuing the thought of knowing who we are and knowing our purpose is one of the greatest quests that every individual wants to master. All these factors play a part collectively in finding your TRUE identity in this world. Well, for me, this has been my story since I can remember, and as I reflect, I can't help but notice that the odds were stacked against me.

Born in Tampa, Florida, but raised in Jacksonville, Florida, I found myself being a product of a broken home that was caused by a divorce. Raised only by my mother, my brother and I were forced to take on the challenge of growing up as men without a father.

As a young boy, it created this opposition of competing to do everything my father did, but the goal was to be better than him. He played football, so my desire was to play and create expectations that would supersede his glory days with my success on the field.

I didn't know as a child that I was living a life with no knowledge of my identity because I was trying to be someone who could erase the hurt and fight to receive affirmation and attention. This pain and drive that was created by my father's absence sent me in a spiral that resulted in me being homeless, facing two near-death experiences, and a setback of self-discovery.

My father wasn't the only piece to the puzzle that caused me to struggle with my identity, but it was the main piece that led me to a place of vulnerability. That place led me to seek out older men like coaches, pastors, and mentors to be a father figure to me. Even then, it was not enough because of the hard times I had to endure throughout my childhood and teenage years.

During the majority of my high school years, I had to take the school and the city bus because my mom worked numerous jobs while going to school just to take care of my brother and me. In my sophomore year in high school, I had rolled my ankle badly at football practice and had to get crutches.

In the same week, my mother, who was overwhelmed by the stress of working and going to school, had received a letter of eviction telling us to leave our apartment. I remember having to hobble up the hotel stairs with my crutches, eating sandwiches for dinner and lunch while I was in school. This went on until my mom let my aunt know about our living situation – we didn't know where we were going to lay our heads from day to day. My aunt moved us in with her.

Moments like this remind me that adversity gives people encouragement to grow, whether it's positive or negative. As for me, it was my drive to turn a negative situation into a positive one.

While I was on crutches I couldn't practice, so I had to look outside of football and ponder, *If the game was ever taken away from me, what would I do, and who would I be?*

At a young age, I was blessed to come into a position of knowing the importance of having a relationship with God. It was my faith that kept me throughout all the ups and downs, learning to find my way as a boy trying to become a man. My faith and who I was at the time was tested during the summer going into my senior year in high school. I got into a heated dispute over a game of football with a young man in the neighborhood. As the tension escalated, the young man and I got into a physical altercation. I notice that the guy backed off, and I was ready to leave for a 7-on-7 summer football practice. As I walked to gather my football gear on my aunt's porch, my cousin told me that there was blood on my shirt. My first thought was *how is that even possible? No one was bleeding.*

My mom walked up to me and started crying, and I didn't understand the tears she was shedding. As I reached out to hug my mom, I started feeling weak, and before I embraced her, I noticed blood everywhere from the walkway to the porch stairs. At that moment, I realized that the sharp pinch that I felt when the young man punched me near my lower back on the left side was actually a stab wound.

Lying on my aunt's porch bleeding out, I remember thinking and saying, "I'm going to die. I'm going to die." My aunt told me to be quiet as she took a bunch of towels and put it to my side to the stop the bleeding as we waited for the ambulance to come get me. Fighting for my life, I realized that it was more to life than what I focused on.

My youth and my identity became the two factors that caused my faith to push through and for me to ask God to give me another chance at life. When he did, the tables of life were reset, and before I left the hospital, I had the opportunity to see and talk to my father.

We reconciled, but my identity was something that I would have to continue to find. The factors that formed my identity at that point in my life was my relationship with God, football, and family. The doctors told my mom and me that I wasn't going to be able to play ball again. A week and a half later, I was back on the field, and for the first time, it seemed like everything was falling into place. I was ready for this moment as I walked across the stage at my high school graduation; there was a sense of joy that I accomplished something that could have been taking away from me.

With no football offers from any colleges, it put me in a position where I had to stay in Jacksonville for my freshmen year at Edward Waters College. Then, after finishing one semester at EWC with a 3.2 GPA, I decided to drop out of college to pray and think about what I wanted to do with my life. The work I was putting into football was not bearing any fruit like with my peers who were having great success in football on the Division 1 level as freshmen.

At the age of 18, I was questioning, "What defines a man when it comes to identity?" I was stuck in life, and my biggest fear at the time was remaining in a place of no progress and growth. I was ready to climb, but I didn't have the right gear, and I never had the right teaching.

In that moment of being out of college, I reconnected with the sources of inspiration that sparked my drive to be successful which were my mom and aunt's investment in me, my city, family, personal story, and the type of legacy I wanted to leave for the next generation. I developed a mindset to have no excuses because there are others who have legitimate reasons to give up on life, but they kept going forward.

This was the beginning of recognizing that God was using my pain, rejections, failures, and inspirations to birth my identity. My fight for identity was won through my relationship with God, helping and encouraging people to know that their stories matter, and having the knowledge that a person will continue to grow and discover who they are until the day they depart from this world.

I'm learning that success is not determined by your accolades, the number of degrees you acquired, the car you drive, or money in the bank but through personal growth. I overcame all of my obstacles because of the lessons that God used life to teach me.

I transferred to numerous of schools, and eventually, I worked hard and received my Associate of Arts degree in journalism at Santa Fe College, and I have recently obtained my Bachelor of Science degree in telecommunications from the University of Florida.

I took on all the hardships and transformed that negativity into positive energy so I could help all kids, even the ones who society considers underprivileged. As I volunteer and help the young boys and girls, I'm reminded that the youth of today is our bright future for tomorrow.

I have younger cousins who I tell, "It's not how you start; it's how you finish. So, be true to you and finish strong. I overcame to give back, and that's my victory. I enjoy spending time with my family, listening to music, and living a fit life. Success is knowing yourself as you grow and develop into your identity, which leads you to live a successful life.

To all the men out there, remember this encouragement in Ecclesiastes 9:11: "That the race is not to the swift, nor the battle to the strong, nor does food come to the wise or wealth to the brilliant or favor to the learned; but time and chance happen to them all."

....

BIO

My name is Hayward Renard Miller Jr. I'm a Florida native born in Tampa and raised in Jacksonville. I live in Gainesville, Florida, with my beautiful wife of four years, Christian D. Miller. I've played organized football for eight years from middle school until my sophomore year in college. I obtained my Associate of Arts degree in journalism at Santa Fe College and my Bachelor of Science degree in telecommunications at the University of Florida in Gainesville. Currently, I work at a Best Buy store as an inventory specialist. I've interned at R.A.W.E. (Reaching Athletes With Education) Recruits as a sports reporter writing sports articles, conducting interviews with local and national talents in sports, filming games, and working social media outlets in Gainesville.

706-284-8405
Facebook: Hayward Miller Jr.
Twitter: @_HaywardMiller
LinkedIn: Hayward Miller Jr.
Instagram: haywardmiller
Snapchat: hmillerjr10

17

A Kid from Compton

By Sherman Turntine

I was just like any other kid in my neighborhood in Compton, California, in the 1960s and '70s. The block I lived on was one big family. We looked after each other, from one end of Central Avenue to the other. We used to play in the front yards, ride our bikes down the street, and wave and say hello to neighbors. Those were the days of community love. But don't get me wrong, we all had our shares of struggles and challenges.

My parents divorced when I was a young boy, but I never wanted for anything. Mom and Dad always made me feel special and loved. My dad stayed active in my life until the day he went home with the Lord. He was once my youth football coach and was a fun-loving, family man and deacon at the church. Sports played a big role in my life, starting from the day my dad gave me a Los Angeles Rams uniform. I would run around the yard and play tackle football with my dog. I later got involved in youths sports, playing football and basketball.

Sports taught me a lot about determination, setting goals, and working with others for a common cause. A lot of my friends played sports. It was one way to keep us busy and off the streets and away from the gang life that started to take root in the '70s in Southern California. To be honest, you could not avoid the gangs in the neighborhood. Most of us tried to steer clear of them and not become a target. Sports provided us with a positive outlet. My block would play kids from other streets in football on a stretch of grass at Caldwell Elementary School.

Caldwell was just down the street from our house. And some of my friends had basketball rims above their garages in the alley. That's where you would find most of us, playing basketball in the alley. The alley became our place of refuge. We would race mini-bikes in the alley, having all kinds of fun right behind our houses.

Some of my coaches became important people in my life growing up. Mr. Robert Davis, who was friends with my dad, was a role model for a lot of young boys, many who didn't have fathers at home. He made us feel important, worthy of something great. I remember one year we went to play a team in Salt Lake City, Utah. For most of us, including myself, we had never been in the snow. Each of us stayed at another player's home. I'll never forget the warm greeting I received from my host family. The Utah player had a mini hockey rink in his basement where I learned a few pointers about the game. We had so much fun riding snowmobiles and playing in the snow… Many of us still talk about that trip to this day. It opened our eyes to a world outside of our neighborhood and introduced us to kind and generous people from different walks of life.

As I grew older, gangs and drugs swept up many of my friends in Compton. I continued to play sports and stayed *neutral.* I will admit, you had to *look the part* and wear certain clothing and colors to avoid becoming a target of gang violence in the neighborhood. Many of my family members were concerned about me. Life in the neighborhood became a little more dangerous in the early '70s. So at the suggestion of my mother and other family members, I went to live with my grandmother in Long Beach, a neighboring city. I considered it to be one of the best moves of my life. Don't get me wrong, LBC had its share of social issues too. But, living with my grandmother and other family members changed my life.

My grandmother taught me so much. She was a great woman. Watching her take care of my grandfather and work as a nurse and barber instilled so much pride in me. She taught me humility and respect for others. I went to Long Beach Poly High School where my mother's brothers, Donald and GG, also went to school. (Poly has a proud tradition in sports.)

One year during high school, my grandmother would work a graveyard shift at St. Mary's Hospital and then come home and fix me a hot breakfast every morning before I headed to school. I admit, I was spoiled a bit. I was indeed thankful and grateful for all she did for me. Grandmother also went deep-sea fishing and had the most beautiful flower and vegetable gardens. I spent many days with her in the gardens tending the plants. She was a woman of the Scripture and would fall asleep in her favorite chair with the Bible in her lap. She read the Bible every night. I know she prayed for all of us each and every day.

I played football at Poly High, where my Uncle Donald was a legendary coach in football and track. Uncle Don is like a second father to me. Just like my parents and grandmother, he has supported me from Day 1. He has been a driving force and role model in my life to this day. He was even-handed. When I got in trouble, he would let me have it and thank me for doing something good. He helped keep me in line during my high school years. Uncle Don was the first to tell me I was "going to college." Uncle Don is a humble man; he's not one to boast about his many accomplishments from being named NFL High School Coach of the Year and his many California state track awards. He pushed his student-athletes in the classroom and on the field; he always taught education first. Uncle Don and my late Aunt Carol will always be special people in my life. They taught me about giving back and love of community. Their house was always open to family and friends.

I started getting interested in writing when I was at Walton Junior High School in Compton. I had good penmanship and liked writing poems. When I moved on to Poly High in Long Beach, I got involved with the student newspaper, *High Life*, and the yearbook staff. My English teacher Mrs. Green encouraged me to pursue my journalism dreams. So on the suggestions of my Uncle Don and others, I hit the books and started thinking about college, in my senior year, mind you. That's when I began to receive athletic scholarships.

I settled on Cal Poly San Luis Obispo; another good decision for me. I picked Cal Poly because it's along the Central Coast of California, midway between Long Beach/Compton/Los Angeles and the San Francisco Bay Area, where I have many family members. I also chose SLO because of its football and journalism programs. Cal Poly, at the time, was a Division II school in football. I felt I would have a better chance of getting more time on the playing field. I considered myself a good football player, but I knew it would take more dedication to play at the next level. On the other side, I got completely involved in the journalism department, writing for the college newspaper. I was lucky to meet two professors who took the time to mentor me and help me plan my coursework. I am truly thankful to Mr. Hayes and Mr. Zuchelli. I wouldn't have made it without their guidance and support.

My college football coaches were also important to my development. My defensive back coach, Coach Sanderson, pushed us hard on the field. He was genuinely concerned about us off the field too. He would invite us over for BBQs at his house. All of the other players on the team were jealous of our close-knit group. Our head coach, Coach Harper, was small in stature but big in motivation. We were really close as teammates, living in the jock dorms... Yes, it got a little wild, and I soon realized that I had to go from practice to dinner, straight to the library, and then to the dorm. If you went to the dorm after dinner, you might not make it to the library.

I spent five years in college after redshirting my first year of football eligibility. The extra time allowed me to hone my journalism skills and intern at the local *Tribune* newspaper. I really enjoyed my time at the city newspaper. It felt good seeing my byline in the newspaper.

Graduation was an emotional and proud time for me. My mother and other family members came to witness the occasion. I felt so humbled and thankful for all the people who helped me get to that point. My grandmother smiled with pride as we posed for pictures. She was one of the people who raised me and encouraged me the most all through high school. It was a great feeling knowing that their hard work over the years was paying off with me graduating.

After graduation, I contacted my dad, who was living in Texarkana, Arkansas. I decided newspaper work was what I wanted to do, and I put away the football cleats. I eventually got a job at the Texarkana Gazette as a copy editor and later wrote a Sunday news column. I was the first black person hired in the newsroom – another proud moment for me and my family.

A few years later, dad had a stroke, and we decided to return to Southern California so he could be close to his sisters and immediate family. I stayed by his side in Los Angeles and continued to pursue newspaper editing work.

I have worked at some major newspapers in my thirty-plus years in the business, including the *Los Angeles Herald Examiner*, *Long Beach Press-Telegram*, *Los Angeles Times*, and the *San Jose Mercury News*. Recently, I hung up my newspaper hat and decided to start my own editing business (I also work for an educational tech startup, a public relations firm in Oakland, California, and a book publishing company). It has been a transition, and I am thankful for all the great people I met in the newspaper industry. Many have groomed me for this moment.

So, I walk out on faith and the lessons learned by the village that raised and mentored me through the years. They all hold a special place in my heart. Each day I hope I make them proud of the life I live. Both of my parents, my dear grandmother, some of my youth sports coaches, and my two college professors are no longer here on Earth. However, I feel their presence, and I give thanks to all of them for showing love and support to a young kid *straight outta Compton.*

I am forever humble and thankful! I was taught to share your knowledge and give back. I truly believe we rise by lifting others.

....

BIO

Sherman Turntine is the founder and owner of Turntine Editing Services. He also works for the educational tech startup Newsela, is the communications director at LA Jones & Associates in Oakland, California, and a copy editor at 7 House Media. Sherman worked over thirty years in the newspaper industry before starting his own business. He is in the process of launching a website and a Facebook page for his business. His work includes editing copy for a number of authors and *Huffington Post* contributors. He lives with his wife in San Jose, California.

shturntine@gmail.com
www.linkedin.com/in/sherman-turntine-917a27b6/

18

Many Tribes, but One Nation

By M. Rasheed

"Listen, bruh," I was told (that may have been the first time I was ever called "bruh"). "I don't know who you think you are, but you need to slow your roll. That's not how we do things here." The firm check from the moderator at the Museum of Black Superheroes made me pause.

Hmm, I thought. *How they did things seemed to be framed within that humorless, pretentious, mask of self-importance that the Afrocentric 'hotep' community was known for.* As far as I was concerned, providing a few spontaneous jokes and respectfully, but gamely, pushing back against their assertions to ignite a spirited dialogue wasn't going to hurt anyone. (Okay, so "jokes" may be pushing it, but "corny-puns-at-the-Mod's-expense-when-he-wanted-his-patriarchal-themes-in-Afrofuturism-topic-to-be-taken-seriously" didn't really flow well in the story.) It was the "who you think you are" part that made me pause. *Were we not in a pro-Black discussion forum set aside by/for lack speculative fiction fans? I'M pro-Black. I'M a Black speculative fiction fan. I thought I was one of YOU.* Those were my inner thoughts.

I was left to reflect on how often I'd been accused by my wife of stubbornness for a reason, and I didn't allow my relatively off-putting 2005 introduction to the Museum of Black Superheroes message board regulars to "slow my roll," as the moderator said. I eventually won over the Afrocentrics among them (to a greater or lesser degree). I even got my younger brother to join the group and bear witness to an increase in membership, fun artistic collaborations, and fellowship. What I didn't know at the time, was how powerful that "who you think you are" line was and how deeply it buried itself in my mind for over a decade.

I realize it is normal for people to spend a certain amount of time wrestling with their self-identity, and I've certainly done so both as an artist and as an African-American. I grew up in Detroit, Michigan, in a home with two pro-Black parents and with my dad being a sit-in demonstrator from the Civil Rights Era; I was no stranger to the Afrocentric, hotep-like language. My problem was that I felt entitled to use the "Black Card" by virtue of all of that ... or even just because. *I'm Black, right? I have Black parents and a Black wife, right? Okay, then gimme my card!* I found out the hard way that the world doesn't work that way. Or, more accurately, my community doesn't work that way.

Despite the above display of my credentials, my parents weren't keen on having me mingle in the local community during my childhood. They held my siblings and I close, and when the so-called "War on Drugs" was heralded by President Ronald Reagan suspiciously announcing the not-yet-arrived crack infestation into urban neighborhoods, my parents moved the family out onto some land in rural Michigan. As fun as our farm years were, the major benefit to me was it enabled me to get a strong grasp on my artistic side. It was then that I developed the rudimentary skills needed to become a professional cartoonist which I later honed in my college BFA program. Without peers to interact with regularly (only my immediate family), a natural propensity for sitting quietly for hours pushing lead-pencil tips around on paper, and an unquenchable love for comics, animated cartoons and superheroes, I developed many of the traits commonly ascribed to the Black Nerd introvert.

During my early college days, I remember hanging out with a talented entrepreneur who ran a custom art airbrushing business in the heart of Detroit. After talking to me for less than ten minutes, he confidently proclaimed that I had grown up in a very sheltered environment with only the television as my window to the outside world. I sat stunned for several seconds, unable to respond. That was the first time I experienced having my "mail read" so accurately.

"Your husband is so quiet," my wife often hears. Of course, as is often the case within my Black Nerd sub-demographic, I didn't *feel* quiet...not with all the cosmos-spanning-world-building going on behind my eyes. I also absolutely did not feel the "Why are you talking White?" nonsense I would hear from my peers around my neighborhood, and I added that to the brewing pot of tools I continuously negotiated with in figuring out my identity.

It didn't take me long to seize the artistic side of myself – the focused training of my education, plus my twenty titled accomplishments as a graphic novel serialist helped with that part. The Muslim side of me was also easy to grasp; I have no desire to imagine a life without God (it would be a waste of my creative talents). But the Black American side of me? That took some real digging.

When I was younger, I thought "Blackness" was as simple as what the White Hollywood executives projected in movies: Just clench a fist and say "Right on, my brotha/sista. I'm Black. That's our thing. Look at me. Come on." It's NOT that simple as it turns out, for both good and for bad. The African-American does not function as a hive-minded swarm with all of us thinking, behaving, liking, and loving all the same things for all the same reasons. It's a good thing that the White Hollywood exec's summation of all I am as a Black American is wrong (as shown in Robert Townsend's courageously brilliant "Hollywood Shuffle"). I'm more than just the dismissed handful of caricatures he needs me to be in his films; I'm composed of several tribes – each with their ideologies, hopes, dreams – connected in a shared history as the Original Human of the Species.

It's only a bad thing in the sense that, since I've been born (1970), the different tribes have been even less connected than they have ever been. We've lost the sense that we HAVE to do everything together to survive because someone told us we didn't have to be that way anymore. They told us that it was okay to abandon ours to become a support class inside of theirs. Personally, I don't think the people who gave us that message were our friends. Despite the differences in how the tribes see the world, in those days, we were still better able to come together to win milestone and empowerment victories along the path of the journey.

I was uneasy during my college years, and for some time afterward, wondering which one of the tribes was "authentically Black." It was the coming to terms with the demonically offensive, "Why are you talking White?" inquiry that finally cured me of that kind of thinking. All of the tribes are authentically Black; all of them make up the nation, and all of them represent our collective truth. Our story is fully told with the very real contributions of the leather-fisted activist, the dashiki-garbed Afrocentric, the suited Black Republican, the striving poor, the legacy wealth accrued elitist, the ambitiously focused ballplayer, the HBCU scholar, and even the quiet Black Nerd artist. No one has the right to tell any of them whether they are really Black or not. They all are. Equally.

Forming my self-identity, I would have that *Candid & Courageous Conversation* with myself and wrestle with the war inside of me. The combatants were two – composed of the proud artist decorated with his independent plumage signifying his embrace of the loner archetype on one side (needed in order to create the time-consuming content that represents my life work). On the other side of that inner fight, there was the person who was once called "bruh" when he dared to challenge a fellow Nerd who self-identified within the Black Tribe of Afrocentrists. That version of me genuinely had his feelings hurt during that encounter because he thought the Black Superhero Fan/Cartoonist was his own tribe, and he had finally come home. It turns out that wasn't a thing, and even though "Black Superhero

Fan/Cartoonist" is a specialty category of my subgroup, it wasn't its own mini-tribe. It was just a loose and fun category of interest for the members of the true tribes who happened to like those things to come together on. I found out then that the Black Nerd identity we all celebrated wasn't strong enough to overpower the tribal lines that were of more substance. So to my then confused shock, I found myself as the he's-so-quiet guy again in that group. Disappointed, I wondered aloud to my wife, "How could this BE?!" I didn't even know that this was something that I wanted, and now looking back, I'm sure it was something I should not have wanted.

My quasi-fantasy vision for that group of Black Nerds was of a tribe of proud men and women who were the spec-fiction lovers' version of the Malcolm X's and Angela Davises of the 1960s but expressed OUR way. The "OUR way" was just in my head ("MY way"). When they expressed our way, it was always from within the clearly defined boundaries of their traditional tribes with the cliques, bickering, and attacks pulled from beefs as old as the African-American ethnic group itself. I found myself content to pretend the group was what I fantasized it to be until that message board eventually faded away, its members disbanding and fading into the social media-verse.

Since then, I briefly flirted with an "If you build it, they will come" forum of my own, but my wife's insistence that I just be myself cured me of all of that. That is the healthiest place to be, and just doing me as a lone artist is the most authentic me. I watch members of the dominant tribe tell others that they are wrong for living their authentic truths when they dare to express themselves from their own unique cultural perspectives either as members of rival tribes or as loners, and I for one recognize it as wrong.

It is wrong for anybody to tell anyone else who is truly Black and who is not. This is the tribe that turned "the struggle" into a totem that they prefer to feed tribute, instead of actively working to close it out. Personally, I am less interested in the empty dance of joining the struggle as a tribe ideology than I am in definitively working for the glory of the Victory of Black Empowerment & Economic Inclusion that I was naively under the impression we were all supposed to want.

According to the dominant Black tribe's actions and rhetoric, you're not Black unless you are wearing the stereotypical colorful, charismatic, and cool plumage while feeding the totem of the struggle. I watched with a fascinated smirk as former President Barack Obama performed his Black walk with his Black handshakes and made Black Power fist clenches after having read about his struggles while trying to come to grips with his identity when raised by White grandparents and a White mom in his memoirs.

Would he have been any less Black if he had not displayed the artificial plumage the most insufferable Black tribe insists we all wear to prove our Blackness? Of course, he would have. Of course. Blackness is beyond the ideology of any one tribe. We all encompass it and define it by our nature, not our *cool* walk.

From underneath my own plume of independence, yet well within the body of my Black Nation, I've decided that it is perfectly fine for me as an artist to incorporate the recognized elements of Afrofuturism into my works without needing the official label, authentication, or problematic baggage of any tribe. It's still Black Art, and if it matches the description of anything, then that's what it is, even well after it inevitably ceases to exist as a movement because of their ham-fisted, over-consciousness about it as such.

I've decided that it's okay just to be me, a tribe of one.

That's who I can confidently say that I am twelve years after that moderator's rhetorical wonderings. That's who we all should be whether we happen to fit neatly into one of the many tribes or not. No matter what, just be the most authentic you because your place within our nation is secure, and no one can take that away from you.

BIO

Muhammad Rasheed is a graphic novel serialist and publisher of original cartoon books under his Second Sight Graphix company. A highly prolific cartoonist, M. Rasheed is known for his two action-packed, 10-title graphic novel series, *Tales of Sinanju: The Destroyer*, and the award-winning *Monsters 101*.

213-457-3324
mrasheed@mrasheed.com
7413 Six Forks Road #207
Raleigh, North Carolina 27615
www.mrasheed.com

19

Agent of Change

By Dale Brown

My story is about the time I evolved from a community safety activist — a liaison to the police department — to a ***proactive agent of change.***

I was living in an area of Detroit, Michigan, near a community known as "Crack Alley." This area got its name because it was an impoverished, predominately African-American community that was known to be a hub for crack cocaine trafficking and violent crimes. Around this time, there were approximately 300, 911 calls and at least one homicide per month, as well as home invasions every single day in one square block.

I, along with my students from my self-defense school that I created, volunteered to protect the community. The building owners agreed to provide us with free apartments, a small financial stipend for expenses, and the legal right to enforce rules for their property. Our community public safety, volunteer initiative encompassed ten buildings and contained around 400 individual dwellings.

I was scared. Two days prior, after interfering with the operation of a local drug dealer, I was threatened by an African-American police sergeant. He said if I were ever to be caught interfering with a drug dealer's operation again that he would come and take my guns.

As benign as that may sound, "taking guns" was a metaphor for something much deeper. It meant that he would come after me. This was a big deal. After all, *how could I help families if I was simultaneously having problems with the police?*

But the next day, around 3 p.m., something happened.

I heard screaming. On the corner of Holcomb and East Jefferson, I saw a swarm of women kicking, clawing, and circling their prey like a pack of wolves.

As I approached, I noticed that they were beating a young girl who I recognized from one of the buildings protected by my volunteers. Her name was Jasmine, and she was 14 years old. At the time, Jasmine was sexually pursued by a 30-year-old man who was in a relationship with a bisexual woman who happened to be a member of an adult lesbian gang. This woman and her fellow gang members decided to attack Jasmine and her family to teach them a lesson.

Before beating Jasmine, they first grabbed her sister and brother, ages two and five respectively, and slammed their skulls into their apartment door. Upon seeing this, Jasmine rushed them inside and was inundated by attacks from the large group of women. She could have either tried to save her siblings or save herself. The gang then proceeded to take her outside and beat her on the street in broad daylight.

My instinct was to break up the fight, but no, I couldn't do that. The police sergeant warned me about getting involved in any altercations outside of the grounds of the private property where we were authorized by the owners to enforce safety protocols. Angering the police could do irreparable damage to the public safety initiative that we were doing in the community. So, I called 911.

Fifteen minutes later, and the police were still not there. The gang was still kicking Jasmine around with no one to stop them. I had to end this…but I couldn't. If I got in trouble with the police, I wouldn't be able to protect all the other people in the community.

Fifteen more minutes went by, still no police. At this point, I had called the police multiple times, and they informed me that they were already aware of the situation, had received many other calls by other witnesses, and that I should stop calling.

Finally, 45 minutes after the assault began, I watched one of the women swing a liquor bottle at Jasmine's head that barely missed her and broke on the ground next to her beaten body. They then sprayed corrosive pesticides in her eyes and face burning her flesh and swelling her orifices. They proceeded to head home into one of our protective buildings leaving Jasmine on the street screaming.

Since they lived in the building for which we protected, I was delighted to find that some of their information was on the rent roll. While a local store owner, Saruk, took Jasmine into his shop to wash her eyes, I called an ambulance.

Eventually, two hours after the assault began and well after Jasmine had been taken to the hospital, two Caucasian police officers arrived. Before I could even fully explain what happened, they asked, "Where is the victim?"

"The victim is in the hospital," I said. "Have her mother take her to the 5th precinct when she gets out," they instructed me.

"Well, don't you want to take down a report?" I asked. "No, we can't because there is no victim here, so there is nothing we can do," they responded.

I insisted, "Can't you find out which hospital she is at and go there?" To which they responded, "No, no, our radios don't reach the hospital," and drove off.

The next day when Jasmine was released from the hospital, I approached her mother. Jasmine's mother was a hardworking woman. She had multiple jobs to take care of her children. Looking at her, I could see the resemblance to her daughter, but I also saw a deep sorrow, stress, and exhaustion on her face.

I told her, "We need to go to the police department to make a report. I have some of the names, addresses, birthdays, and phone numbers of the attackers. I can provide their information to law enforcement."

"I'm not going to press charges," she said curtly.

"Why not!" I exclaimed.

"What do you mean why not?" She asked in a slightly surprised tone. "You're not from Detroit, are you?"

Shocked, I said, "I'm from Ann Arbor, but it doesn't matter where I'm from! Going to the police is the right thing to do. The problem with Detroit is people like you who won't cooperate with law enforcement and won't help police help them. All you have to do is your part as a good citizen and a good mother."

Hearing the accusatory tone in my voice, she backed off speaking quieter and said, "The police aren't going to do anything."

I said, "Listen, you do your part, and the police will do theirs. You just have to do what they say. You have to agree to prosecute, and cooperate with the investigators."

Frustrated, she said, "No, it's not going to work!"

Sensing that I still did not understand, she explained, "It doesn't do any good."

I stated, "The police are going to prosecute your daughter's attackers. We have most of their information, and I am a witness. If you are a good mother, you will file charges with the police department."

She cried, "I can't do it! I can't do it!"

"Think about your daughter; you need to do this for her. If you don't take this to the police, her beating will be on your hands," I replied.

Finally, distraught, her mother agreed, "Fine, I'll go."

I was so proud. I was now going to be able to show a direct correlation between legal action and civilized behavior. The gang of women was not civilized, but we could make a difference by following the rules and working with law enforcement. Kids who saw the girl get attacked would also see that the women went to prison for doing it. Justice would be served, and faith would be restored in the justice system and civilization in general.

When we arrived at the 5th precinct police station, I was excited because the sergeant at the desk was a woman. I thought *she is a black woman, approximately the same age as Jasmine's mother. And she is from Detroit. She is going to help Jasmine and her mother because they are also black females from Detroit.* I was filled with joy as I approached the desk because we were finally going to show the kids in the neighborhood that working with police will make the community a safer and more civilized place.

When I got to the desk, I said, "My name is Dale Brown, and I provide security for the..." and before I could even finish, in a loud, aggressive tone she said, "Are you related to the victim?"

"No, ma'am," I replied. "THEN BACK AWAY FROM MY DESK," she yelled in a derogatory, commanding tone.

As soon as she raised her voice, Jasmine started whimpering a little bit from beneath the mountains of bandages wrapped around her face looking at me.

I said, "No, don't cry! The officer is going to help you." Jasmine and her mother looked at me with fear in their eyes, and the sergeant said, "I SAID BACK UP, NOW" in a condescending, aggressive and disrespectful tone.

Jasmine's mother began to explain, "She just got out of the hospital after she was attacked..."

The sergeant aggressively interrupted by asking, "Attacked by who?"

"Attacked by people from our apartment building," replied Jasmine's mother softly.

"WHERE WAS YOU? YOU HER MOTHER! AIN'T YOU?" demanded the sergeant, as if the blame was to be placed on the minor child victim and her mother.

"Uh..." As Jasmine's mother was gathering her thoughts, the sergeant yelled, "SPEAK UP!"

At this point, Jasmine broke down into tears, which irritated the sergeant as she continued to berate and scold her and her mother.

Jasmine began to gasp for air as she sobbed, showing outward signs of deep emotional trauma that was being amplified by public humiliation in the lobby of the police station…while I stood helpless. The entire time, they were being degraded and treated as if they were a nuisance. This was when I looked into Jasmine's mother's eyes as she looked into mine. I could see that she was defenseless and humiliated. As was I. That was the moment that changed my life forever. I felt emotionally traumatized and mentally scarred by what I had done to this family by forcing them against their will to go to a police station where they knew offered them no refuge or protection.

I was heartbroken. Jasmine, an innocent 14-year-old girl who was violently beaten after seeing her siblings assaulted, was now being insulted by the police. She was sobbing continuously underneath the bandages that covered all of her face except her mouth and one eye.

After we had left the police station, I gave them a ride home. We didn't say much on the way back. I could sense the feeling of despair in the air. I was wrong and Jasmine's mother — who had taken a full day off of work to do this — was right.

She was not what was wrong with Detroit; I was. I stood by and let my self-survival get in the way while Jasmine was ruthlessly beaten. I could have stopped it, but I didn't. To make matters worse, I shamed a loving mother to the point that she had to put her child and herself through even more trauma, and possibly more risk, than they had already experienced. I swore and pledged that I would never allow anyone to be harmed around me, no matter what; I would rather die than allow harm to come to others. Since that day, 23 years ago, I've never allowed anyone to be harmed again by my action or inaction!

....

BIO

Dale Brown is the founder and director of the Detroit Threat Management Training Center – a community and corporate protective services non-governmental organization (NGO). The organization is looking for support to open training centers internationally to make the world safer through non-violence and the love of humanity!

800.525.3491
www.ThreatManagementCenter.com
www.facebook.com/THREAT.MANAGEMENT.CENTER

20

Part of the Plan

By Chris B. Williams

I remember the day my mother passed away like it was yesterday. My emotions were running rampant as I drove from Sturbridge, Massachusetts to New York City after I received a call from my dad that my mother had passed from a heart attack. WOW! My heartbeat grew louder and harder as I thought, *One of my biggest supporters is gone! This was not part of the plan. Such an unexpected turn. Come on, God, not now!*

Six months before losing my mother I was uprooted from my comfortable life, and new wife, and moved from New York City to Sturbridge, Massachusetts, to continue a once-lucrative sales position.

Although reluctant, I thought this was my only option.

Every Monday morning at 7 a.m. I dreaded our weekly work conference call. I would almost get sick to my stomach. Oftentimes, I would hope and pray that it would be canceled. As I listened to each person on the call explain their plans for the day and how they would strategize to attain more customers, I felt more and more distant. They were genuinely excited and passionate, but I had lost my zest for this work.

I would try to amp myself up, but it just wasn't there anymore. My ideas and suggestions seemed to come from a far-off space galaxy to them. After I had stated my plans for the week, there was often a long deaf pause. It was like, "Uh, ok… Thank you, Chris." No disrespect or offense to anyone on the call, but we were not on the same page.

These conference calls were no doubt a turning point for me. *A blessing in disguise!* My passion and purpose in life needed to be seen, heard, and understood. It no longer could be placed on the back burner. The validation I was seeking was not here; therefore, I had to pursue a different course.

At some point in our lives, we all are faced with making a critical decision.

During this trying time, I decided to reach for my GREATNESS! I decided to stretch myself to the limit and step out of my comfort zone and become a motivational speaker.

So many of us have gifts and talents that can impact the lives of others. Unfortunately, we become complacent and play it safe.

So, what made me decide to become a motivational speaker? I had to be honest with myself. I've always been a speaker. From a very young age, I have had a way with words. I've spoken in church and at schools and had even developed a unique talent for connecting with young people. Expressing myself verbally usually came natural and with ease. I can remember being with my buddies growing up, and they would always appoint me as the spokesperson for the group to gain us an advantage in almost every circumstance or to get us out of a dilemma. To my credit, my success rate was much higher than my failures. As a result, I became extremely confident as a leader and a speaker. Not fully understanding it at the time, I was developing and nurturing my gift.

When I accepted a basketball scholarship to attend Manhattan College in New York City, I knew one thing for sure; my major would be communications. Regardless of what direction my basketball career would take me, communication was my passion. Throughout my four years at Manhattan College, I learned so much about my passion for speaking and communicating on and off the basketball court. The importance of connecting with people verbally and non-verbally quickly became a high priority. This was a common re-occurring theme in all of my classes. It even spilled over to my basketball career.

As the point guard and one of the leaders on the court, I took pride in understanding what my teammates liked and disliked. I was also not afraid to express my expectations of them. Each player had a different emotional makeup and needed to be treated and dealt with according to their emotions and talent. I recognized that in my senior year when I was able to help lead our team to the Metro Atlantic Athletic Conference Championship and a spot in the NCAA Tournament after a 35-year absence in the school's history. Our head coach Fran Fraschilla, a now famed ESPN basketball commentator and analyst, called me the best leader he had ever coached. (Thanks!)

Upon graduating from college, I worked in sales for over twenty years, using my gift sparingly and not to its full potential. Like so many other people, I had become comfortable with my situation. Deep inside I knew I was not truly satisfied. My comfort zone needed to be disrupted. My *man-in-the-mirror* turning point came when I was given a complimentary ticket to attend a speakers' boot camp hosted by one of the leading speakers in the country. I nearly talked myself out of going thinking to myself every reason I shouldn't attend. THANK GOD I did not talk myself out of going. The experience opened my eyes to a whole new world. I was able to see, interact, and hear top speakers in person. They were all so willing to share their insights on how to be successful, and what was so astonishing, I felt they were just like me! The energy was unbelievable! It was contagious, even after the first few hours. That's when I called my wife and told her I wanted to pursue becoming a professional speaker. After attending the boot camp, I soon found out that it wasn't as easy as I thought.

Becoming a top speaker was going to take a lot of hard work and determination, but I knew I was willing to take a risk and follow my passion. All the signs were pointing in that direction. There began to be no better feeling than the ability to help someone feel good about themselves.

With complete humility, my goal is to change the world. I believe this 100 percent! My mother and I had numerous conversations about my pursuing a dream of becoming a world-renowned public speaker. I could always envision myself on stage speaking to crowds of people impacting their lives. My passion was overwhelming me, and I had to start moving in the direction of my dreams. Through pursuing my purpose, I experienced life, growth, and true service; a hallmark of what my mother had always taught me.

Today, I stand before many as a Motivational Speaker and Positive Energy Coach. With the assistance of my beautiful wife and a tremendous support system of family and friends, I am able to live my passion and purpose every day. I continue to encourage the masses to surround yourself with people who fully believe in you because it will increase your value. Through trials and tribulations, it has become crystal clear what my purpose is: To make people feel good and be an agent of Positive Change.

I am incredibly blessed to travel around the country speaking at schools, conferences, and corporations. A significant highlight is when people come up to me and say how much my speaking has inspired them. The gratitude and expressions are priceless.

I can recall one particular high school student who approached me. This young man was in the twelfth grade. He sat all the way in the back of the auditorium; the least likely person one would expect to say anything while exiting the stage. As I was on my way out of the school, this young man approached me and told me he was on the verge of giving up. He wanted to know what made me do what I do. I simply told him, "I'm here to help." His response was classic. He said, "You give me hope!" This made my day because we all need hope.

I believe I receive much more than I give when I travel throughout the country speaking. Some of my experiences are remarkable. I am consistently learning something new every day. I always say everyone likes to be appreciated, and I truly believe this. When you feel you add value to something it breeds confidence.

As I sit writing this on a relaxing flight from New York to Chicago en-route to speak at a Fortune 500 company, all I can do is smile. The joy from my grin has nothing to do with my flight but more so a thank you to my mom and support system for encouraging me to pursue *OUR DREAM*! Now, I realize this was all part of the plan.

....

BIO

As a Positive Energy Coach, motivational speaker, entrepreneur, and mentor, Chris B. Williams captivates his audience with an optimistic outlook on life. Whether working with teenagers, college students, athletes, organizations, or anyone seeking inspiration, he engages and elevates everyone he encounters.

For Chris, positivity starts at home. Born and raised in Philadelphia, he was an All-City and All-State basketball player before receiving a full scholarship to Manhattan College where he led the team to the MAAC Championships in 1993 and a spot in the NCAA Tournament. Upon graduating with a bachelor's degree in communications, he became a sales representative with Jostens working with students to help them recognize and celebrate their achievements.

Today, Chris draws on these enriching experiences in his personal development programs through his company, Williams Unlimited Inc. Signature offerings include Hear Chris Speak keynotes, the highly interactive and most requested How to Use Positive Energy to Change Your Mindset, Be More Productive and Achieve Ultimate Success, How to Build Stronger Culture in Schools seminars, a comprehensive Journey to Manhood eight-week program, and one-on-one positive energy coaching sessions.

Charismatic, charming, energetic, and always smiling, Chris is an in-demand speaker known for tackling a wide range of topics from living with positivity to leadership, relationships, dreaming big, ethics and professionalism.

Among the many organizations that have already benefited from his words of encouragement are the Disney Dreamers Academy with Steve Harvey, Rutgers University, the New Jersey Institute of Technology (NJIT), the City University of New York (CUNY), Amida Care, the Miami Heat, the New York City Department of Education, and various high schools, colleges, and churches throughout the country. Over the years, he has worked with Cuttino Mobley, Steve Lappas, and Fran Fraschilla and has been featured on ESPN.

Along with teaching others about positivity, working with young people is one of his passions. Community involvement is certainly a priority for Chris, and in 2013, he co-founded the Williams & Bullock Basketball Academy, an organization that helps aspiring athletes to be better players and better people. In addition, he oversees a group called Keeping It Real, which helps teenagers connect spiritual ideals with current events.

A lifelong basketball lover, Chris is also the voice of the Manhattan Jaspers, broadcasting all of the men and women's games on TV and radio.

He resides in Queens, New York with his wife and business manager Leah.

Did you love the book?

Tell the world: #20beautifulmen on all your social media sites and share why you loved it

Made in the USA
Columbia, SC
13 August 2023

21540253R10080